I0536210

THE WINDS
OF TIME

AND OTHER STORIES

MORE WILDSIDE CLASSICS

BY JOHN W. CAMPBELL, JR.
The Black Star Passes
Invaders from the Infinite
Islands of Space

BY LESTER DEL REY
Badge of Infamy
Police Your Planet
The Sky Is Falaling

BY MURRAY LEINSTER
The Aliens and Other Stories
The Black Galaxy
The Brain Stealers
The Duplicators
The Last Spaceship
The Mutant Weapon
Operation: Outer Space
Operation: Terror
The Pirates of Zan
The Planet Explorer
The Runaway Skyscraper and Other Tales
Space Tug
War with the Gizmos

BY ANDRE NORTON
Key Out of Time
Plague Ship
Ralestone Luck
Rebel Spurs
Star Born
Star Hunter
Storm Over Warlock
The Time Traders

OTHER TITLES
Brigands of the Moon, by Ray Cummings
Star Surgeon, by Alan E. Nourse
A Planet for Texans, by H. Beam Piper
The White Sybil, by Clark Ashton Smith

Please see www.wildsidebooks.com for a complete list.

THE WINDS OF TIME

AND OTHER STORIES

JAMES H. SCHMITZ

WILDSIDE PRESS

THE WINDS OF TIME AND OTHER STORIES

Copyright © 2008 by Wildside Press LLC
www.wildsidebooks.com

"An Incident on Route" originally appeared in *Worlds of If*, January 1962. "Watch the Sky" originally appeared in *Analog*, August 1962. "The Winds of Time" originally appeared in *Analog*, September 1962. "Lion Loose" originally appeared in *Analog Science Fiction and Science Fact*, October 1961.

CONTENTS

AN INCIDENT ON ROUTE 12

Phil Garfield was thirty miles south of the little town of Redmon on Route Twelve when he was startled by a series of sharp, clanking noises. They came from under the Packard's hood.

The car immediately began to lose speed. Garfield jammed down the accelerator, had a sense of sick helplessness at the complete lack of response from the motor. The Packard rolled on, getting rid of its momentum, and came to a stop.

Phil Garfield swore shakily. He checked his watch, switched off the headlights and climbed out into the dark road. A delay of even half an hour here might be disastrous. It was past midnight, and he had another hundred and ten miles to cover to reach the small private airfield where Madge waited for him and the thirty thousand dollars in the suitcase on the Packard's front seat.

If he didn't make it before daylight....

He thought of the bank guard. The man had made a clumsy play at being a hero, and that had set off the fool woman who'd run screaming into their line of fire. One dead. Perhaps two. Garfield hadn't stopped to look at an evening paper.

But he knew they were hunting for him.

He glanced up and down the road. No other headlights in sight at the moment, no light from a building showing on the forested hills. He reached back into the car and brought out the suitcase, his gun, a big flashlight and the box of shells which had been standing beside the suitcase. He broke the box open, shoved a handful of shells and the .38 into his coat pocket, then took suitcase and flashlight over to the shoulder of the road and set them down.

There was no point in groping about under the Packard's hood. When it came to mechanics, Phil Garfield was a moron and well aware of it. The car was useless to him now . . . except as bait.

But as bait it might be very useful.

Should he leave it standing where it was? No, Garfield decided. To anybody driving past it would merely suggest a necking party, or a drunk sleeping off his load before continuing home. He might have to wait an hour or more before someone decided to stop. He didn't have the time. He reached in through the window, hauled the top of the steering wheel towards him and put his weight against the rear window frame.

The Packard began to move slowly backwards at a slant across the road. In a minute or two he had it in position. Not blocking the road entirely, which would arouse immediate suspicion, but angled across it, lights out, empty, both front doors open and inviting a passerby's investigation.

Garfield carried the suitcase and flashlight across the right-hand shoulder of the road and moved up among the trees and undergrowth of the slope above the shoulder. Placing the suitcase between the bushes, he brought out the .38, clicked the safety off and stood waiting.

Some ten minutes later, a set of headlights appeared speeding up Route Twelve from the direction of Redmon. Phil Garfield went down on one knee before he came within range of the lights. Now he was completely concealed by the vegetation.

The car slowed as it approached, braking nearly to a stop sixty feet from the stalled Packard. There were several people inside it; Garfield heard voices, then a woman's loud laugh. The driver tapped his horn inquiringly twice, moved the car slowly forward. As the headlights went past him,

Garfield got to his feet among the bushes, took a step down towards the road, raising the gun.

Then he caught the distant gleam of a second set of headlights approaching from Redmon. He swore under his breath and dropped back out of sight. The car below him reached the Packard, edged cautiously around it, rolled on with a sudden roar of acceleration.

The second car stopped when still a hundred yards away, the Packard caught in the motionless glare of its lights. Garfield heard the steady purring of a powerful motor.

For almost a minute, nothing else happened. Then the car came gliding smoothly on, stopped again no more than thirty feet to Garfield's left. He could see it now through the screening bushes — a big job, a long, low four-door sedan. The motor continued to purr. After a moment, a door on the far side of the car opened and slammed shut.

A man walked quickly out into the beam of the head-lights and started towards the Packard.

Phil Garfield rose from his crouching position, the .38 in his right hand, flashlight in his left. If the driver was alone, the thing was now cinched! But if there was some-body else in the car, somebody capable of fast, decisive action, a slip in the next ten seconds might cost him the sedan, and quite probably his freedom and life. Garfield lined up the .38's sights steadily on the center of the ap-proaching man's head. He let his breath out slowly as the fellow came level with him in the road and squeezed off one shot.

Instantly he went bounding down the slope to the road. The bullet had flung the man sideways to the pavement. Garfield darted past him to the left, crossed the beam of the headlights, and was in darkness again on the far side of the road, snapping on his flashlight as he sprinted up to the car.

The motor hummed quietly on. The flashlight showed the seats empty. Garfield dropped the light, jerked both doors open in turn, gun pointing into the car's interior. Then he stood still for a moment, weak and almost dizzy with relief.

There was no one inside. The sedan was his.

The man he had shot through the head lay face down on the road, his hat flung a dozen feet away from him. Route Twelve still stretched out in dark silence to east and west. There should be time enough to clean up the job before anyone else came along. Garfield brought the suitcase down and put it on the front seat of the sedan, then started back to get his victim off the road and out of sight. He scaled the man's hat into the bushes, bent down, grasped the ankles and started to haul him towards the left side of the road where the ground dropped off sharply beyond the shoulder.

The body made a high, squealing sound and began to writhe violently.

Shocked, Garfield dropped the legs and hurriedly took the gun from his pocket, moving back a step. The squealing noise rose in intensity as the wounded man quickly flopped over twice like a struggling fish, arms and legs sawing about with startling energy. Garfield clicked off the safety, pumped three shots into his victim's back.

The grisly squeals ended abruptly. The body continued to jerk for another second or two, then lay still.

Garfield shoved the gun back into his pocket. The unexpected interruption had unnerved him; his hands shook as he reached down again for the stranger's ankles. Then he jerked his hands back, and straightened up, staring.

From the side of the man's chest, a few inches below the

right arm, something like a thick black stick, three feet long, protruded now through the material of the coat.

It shone, gleaming wetly, in the light from the car. Even in that first uncomprehending instant, something in its appearance brought a surge of sick disgust to Garfield's throat. Then the stick bent slowly halfway down its length, forming a sharp angle, and its tip opened into what could have been three blunt, black claws which scrabbled clumsily against the pavement. Very faintly, the squealing began again, and the body's back arched up as if another sticklike arm were pushing desperately against the ground beneath it.

Garfield acted in a blur of horror. He emptied the .38 into the thing at his feet almost without realizing he was doing it. Then, dropping the gun, he seized one of the ankles, ran backwards to the shoulder of the road, dragging the body behind him.

In the darkness at the edge of the shoulder, he let go of it, stepped around to the other side and with two frantically savage kicks sent the body plunging over the shoulder and down the steep slope beyond. He heard it crash through the bushes for some seconds, then stop. He turned, and ran back to the sedan, scooping up his gun as he went past. He scrambled into the driver's seat and slammed the door shut behind him.

His hands shook violently on the steering wheel as he pressed down the accelerator. The motor roared into life and the big car surged forward. He edged it past the Packard, cursing aloud in horrified shock, jammed down the accelerator and went flashing up Route Twelve, darkness racing beside and behind him.

What had it been? Something that wore what seemed to be a man's body like a suit of clothes, moving the body as a man moves, driving a man's car . . . roach-armed, roach-legged itself!

Garfield drew a long, shuddering breath. Then, as he slowed for a curve, there was a spark of reddish light in the rear-view mirror.

He stared at the spark for an instant, braked the car to a stop, rolled down the window and looked back.

Far behind him along Route Twelve, a fire burned. Approximately at the point where the Packard had stalled out, where something had gone rolling off the road into the bushes. . . .

Something, Garfield added mentally, that found fiery automatic destruction when death came to it, so that its secrets would remain unrevealed.

But for him the fire meant the end of a nightmare. He rolled the window up, took out a cigarette, lit it, and pressed the accelerator. . . .

In incredulous fright, he felt the nose of the car tilt upwards, headlights sweeping up from the road into the trees.

Then the headlights winked out. Beyond the windshield, dark tree branches floated down towards him, the night sky beyond. He reached frantically for the door handle.

A steel wrench clamped silently about each of his arms, drawing them in against his sides, immobilizing them there. Garfield gasped, looked up at the mirror and saw a pair of faintly gleaming red eyes watching him from the rear of the car. Two of the things . . . the second one stood behind him out of sight, holding him. They'd been in what had seemed to be the trunk compartment. And they had come out.

The eyes in the mirror vanished. A moist, black roach-arm reached over the back of the seat beside Garfield, picked up the cigarette he had dropped, extinguished it with rather horribly human motions, then took up Garfield's gun and drew back out of sight.

He expected a shot, but none came.

One doesn't fire a bullet through the suit one intends to wear. . . .

It wasn't until that thought occurred to him that tough Phil Garfield began to scream. He was still screaming minutes later when, beyond the windshield, the spaceship floated into view among the stars.

WATCH THE SKY

Uncle William Boles' war-battered old Geest gun gave the impression that at some stage of its construction it had been pulled out of shape and then hardened in that form. What remained of it was all of one piece. The scarred and pitted twin barrels were stubby and thick, and the vacant oblong in the frame behind them might have contained standard energy magazines. It was the stock which gave the alien weapon its curious appearance. Almost eighteen inches long, it curved abruptly to the right and was too thin, knobbed and indented to fit comfortably at any point in a human hand. Over half a century had passed since, with the webbed, boneless fingers of its original owner closed about it, it last spat deadly radiation at human foemen. Now it hung among Uncle William's other collected oddities on the wall above the living room fireplace.

And today, Phil Boles thought, squinting at the gun with reflectively narrowed eyes, some eight years after Uncle William's death, the old war souvenir would quietly become a key factor in the solution of a colonial planet's problems. He ran a finger over the dull, roughened frame, bent closer to study the neatly lettered inscription:

GUNDERLAND BATTLE TROPHY,
ANNO 2172, SGT. WILLIAM G. BOLES.

Then, catching a familiar series of clicking noises from the hall, he straightened quickly and turned away. When Aunt Beulah's go-chair came rolling back into the room, Phil was sitting at the low tea table, his back to the fireplace.

The go-chair's wide flexible treads carried it smoothly down the three steps to the sunken section of the living room, Beulah sitting jauntily erect in it, for all the ninety-six years which had left her the last survivor of the original group of Earth settlers on the world of Roye. She tapped her fingers here and there on the chair's armrests, swinging it deftly about, and brought it to a stop beside the tea table.

"That was Susan Feeney calling," she reported. "And *there* is somebody else for you who thinks I have to be taken care of! Go ahead and finish the pie, Phil. Can't hurt a husky man like you. Got a couple more baking for you to take along."

Phil grinned. "That'd be worth the trip up from Fort Roye all by itself."

Beulah looked pleased. "Not much else I can do for my great-grand nephew nowadays, is there?"

Phil said, after a moment, "Have you given any further thought to —"

"Moving down to Fort Roye?" Beulah pursed her thin lips. "Goodness, Phil, I do hate to disappoint you again, but I'd be completely out of place in a town apartment."

"Dr. Fitzsimmons would be pleased," Phil remarked.

"Oh, him! Fitz is another old worry wart. What he wants is to get me into the hospital. Nothing doing!"

Phil shook his head helplessly, laughed. "After all, working a tupa ranch —"

"Nonsense. The ranch is just enough bother to be interesting. The appliances do everything anyway, and Susan is down here every morning for a chat and to make sure I'm still all right. She won't admit that, of course, but if she thinks something should be taken care of, the whole Feeney family shows up an hour later to do it. There's really no reason for you to be sending a dozen men up from Fort Roye every two months to harvest the tupa."

Phil shrugged. "No one's ever yet invented an easy way

to dig up those roots. And the CLU's glad to furnish the men."

"Because you're its president?"

"Uh-huh."

"It really doesn't cost you anything?" Beulah asked doubtfully.

"Not a cent."

"Hm-m-m. Been meaning to ask you. What made you set up that . . . Colonial Labor Union?"

Phil nodded. "That's the official name."

"Why did you set it up in the first place?"

"That's easy to answer," Phil said. "On the day the planetary population here touched the forty thousand mark, Roye became legally entitled to its labor union. Why not take advantage of it?"

"What's the advantage?"

"More Earth money coming in, for one thing. Of the twelve hundred CLU members we've got in Fort Roye now, seventy-six per cent were unemployed this month. We'll have a compensation check from the Territorial Office with the next ship coming in." He smiled at her expression. "Sure, the boys *could* go back to the tupa ranches. But not everyone likes that life as well as you and the Feeneys."

"Earth government lets you get away with it?" Beulah asked curiously. "They used to be pretty tight-fisted."

"They still are — but it's the law. The Territorial Office also pays any CLU president's salary, incidentally. I don't draw too much at the moment, but that will go up automatically with the membership and my responsibilities."

"What responsibilities?"

"We've set up a skeleton organization," Phil explained. "Now, when Earth government decides eventually to establish a big military base here, they can run in a hundred thousand civilians in a couple of months and everyone will be fitted into the pattern on Roye without trouble or confusion. That's really the reason for all the generosity."

Beulah sniffed. "Big base, my eye! There hasn't been six months since I set foot here that somebody wasn't talking about Fort Roye being turned into a Class A military base pretty soon. It'll never happen, Phil. Roye's a farm planet, and that's what it's going to stay."

Phil's lips twitched. "Well, don't give up hope."

"*I'm* not anxious for any changes," Beulah said. "I like Roye the way it is."

She peered at a button on the go-chair's armrest which had just begun to put out small bright-blue flashes of light. "Pies are done," she announced. "Phil, are you sure you can't stay for dinner?"

Phil looked at his watch, shook his head. "I'd love to, but I really have to get back."

"Then I'll go wrap up the pies for you."

Beulah swung the go-chair around, sent it slithering up the stairs and out the door. Phil stood up quickly. He stepped over to the fireplace, opened his coat and detached a flexible, box-shaped object from the inner lining. He laid this object on the mantle, and turned one of three small knobs about its front edge to the right. The box promptly extruded a supporting leg from each of its four corners, pushed itself up from the mantle and became a miniature table. Phil glanced at the door through which Beulah had vanished, listened a moment, then took the Geest gun from the wall, laid it carefully on top of the device and twisted the second dial.

The odd-looking gun began to sink slowly down through the surface of Phil's instrument, like a rock disappearing in mud. Within seconds it vanished completely;

then, a moment later, it began to emerge from the box's underside. Phil let the Geest gun drop into his hand, replaced it on the wall, turned the third knob. The box withdrew its supports and sank down to the mantle. Phil clipped it back inside his coat, closed the coat, and strolled over to the center of the room to wait for Aunt Beulah to return with the pies.

It was curious, Phil Boles reflected as his aircar moved out over the craggy, plunging coastline to the north some while later, that a few bold minds could be all that was needed to change the fate of a world. A few minds with imagination enough to see how circumstances about them might be altered.

On his left, far below, was now the flat ribbon of the peninsula, almost at sea level, its tip widening and lifting into the broad, rocky promontory on which stood Fort Roye — the only thing on the planet bigger and of more significance than the shabby backwoods settlements. And Fort Roye was neither very big nor very significant. A Class F military base around which, over the years, a straggling town had come into existence, Fort Roye was a space-age trading post linking Roye's population to the mighty mother planet, and a station from which the otherwise vacant and utterly unimportant 132nd Segment of the Space Territories was periodically and uneventfully patrolled. It was no more than that. Twice a month, an Earth ship settled down to the tiny port, bringing supplies, purchases, occasional groups of reassigned military and civilians — the latter suspected of being drawn as a rule from Earth's Undesirable classification. The ship would take off some days later, with a return load of the few local products for which there was outside demand, primarily the medically valuable tupa roots; and Fort Roye lay quiet again.

The planet was not at fault. Essentially, it had what was needed to become a thriving colony in every sense. At fault was the Geest War. The war had periods of flare-up and periods in which it seemed to be subsiding. During the past decade it had been subsiding again. One of the early flare-ups, one of the worst, and the one which brought the war closest to Earth itself, was the Gunderland Battle in which Uncle William Boles' trophy gun had been acquired. But the war never came near Roye. The action was all in the opposite section of the giant sphere of the Space Territories, and over the years the war drew steadily farther away.

And Earth's vast wealth — its manpower, materials and money — was pouring into space in the direction the Geest War was moving. Worlds not a tenth as naturally attractive as Roye, worlds where the basic conditions for human life were just above the unbearable point, were settled and held, equipped with everything needed and wanted to turn them into independent giant fortresses, with a population not too dissatisfied with its lot. When Earth government didn't count the expense, life could be made considerably better than bearable almost anywhere.

Those were the circumstances which condemned Roye to insignificance. Not everyone minded. Phil Boles, native son, did mind. His inclinations were those of an operator, and he was not being given an adequate opportunity to exercise them. Therefore, the circumstances would have to be changed, and the precise time to make the change was at hand. Phil himself was not aware of every factor involved, but he was aware of enough of them. Back on Earth, a certain political situation was edging towards a specific point of instability. As a result, an Earth ship which was not one of the regular freighters had put down at Fort Roye some days before. Among its passengers were Commissioner Sanford of the Territorial Office, a well-known politician, and a Mr. Ronald Black, the popular and enterprising owner of Earth's second largest news outlet system. They were on a joint fact-finding tour of the thinly scattered colonies in this remote section of the Territories, and had wound up eventually at the most remote of all — the 132nd Segment and Roye.

That was one factor. Just visible twenty thousand feet below Phil — almost directly beneath him now as the aircar made its third leisurely crossing of the central belt of the peninsula — was another. From here it looked like an irregular brown circle against the peninsula's nearly white ground. Lower down, it would have resembled nothing so much as the broken and half-decayed spirals of a gigantic snail shell, its base sunk deep in the ground and its shattered point rearing twelve stories above it. This structure, known popularly as "the ruins" in Fort Roye, was supposed to have been the last stronghold of a semi-intelligent race native to Roye, which might have become extinct barely a century before the Earthmen arrived. A factor associated with the ruins again was that their investigation was the passionately pursued hobby of First Lieutenant Norman Vaughn, Fort Roye's Science Officer.

Add to such things the reason Roye was not considered in need of a serious defensive effort by Earth's strategists — the vast distances between it and any troubled area, and so the utter improbability that a Geest ship might come close enough to discover that here was another world as well suited for its race as for human beings. And then a final factor: the instrument attached to the lining of Phil's coat — a very special "camera" which now carried the contact impressions made on it by Uncle William's souvenir gun. Put 'em all together, Phil thought cheerily, and they spelled out interesting developments on Roye in the very near future.

He glanced at his watch again, swung the aircar about and started back inland. He passed presently high above Aunt Beulah's tupa ranch and that of the Feeney family two miles farther up the mountain, turned gradually to the east and twenty minutes later was edging back down the ranges to the coast. Here in a wild, unfarmed region, perched at the edge of a cliff dropping nearly nine hundred feet to the swirling tide, was a small, trim cabin which was the property of a small, trim Fort Roye lady named Celia Adams. Celia had been shipped out from Earth six years before, almost certainly as an Undesirable, though only the Territorial Office and Celia herself knew about that, the Botany Bay aspect of worlds like Roye being handled with some tact by Earth.

Phil approached the cabin only as far as was necessary to make sure that the dark-green aircar parked before it was one belonging to Major Wayne Jackson, the Administration Officer and second in command at Fort Roye — another native son and an old acquaintance. He then turned away, dropped to the woods ten miles south and made a second inconspicuous approach under cover of the trees. There might be casual observers in the area, and while his meeting with Jackson and Celia Adams today revealed nothing in itself, it would be better if no one knew about it.

He grounded the car in the forest a few hundred yards from the Adams cabin, slung a rifle over his shoulder and set off along a game path. It was good hunting territory, and the rifle would explain his presence if he ran into somebody. When he came within view of the cabin, he discovered Celia and her visitor on the covered back patio, drinks standing before them. Jackson was in hunting clothes. Phil remained quietly back among the trees for some seconds watching the two, aware of something like a last-minute hesitancy. A number of things passed slowly through his mind.

What they planned to do was no small matter. It was a hoax which should have far-reaching results, on a gigantic scale. And if Earth government realized it had been hoaxed, the thing could become very unpleasant. That tough-minded central bureaucracy did not ordinarily bother to obtain proof against those it suspected. The suspicion was enough. Individuals and groups whom the shadow of doubt touched found themselves shunted unobtrusively into some backwater of existence and kept there. It was supposed to be very difficult to emerge from such a position again.

In the back of his mind, Phil had been conscious of that, but it had seemed an insignificant threat against the excitement arising from the grandiose impudence of the plan, the perhaps rather small-boyish delight at being able to put something over, profitably, on the greatest power of all. Even now it might have been only a natural wariness that brought the threat up for a final moment of reflection. He didn't, of course, want to incur Earth government's disapproval. But why believe that he might? On all Roye there would be only three who knew — Wayne Jackson, Celia Adams, and himself. All three would benefit, each in a different way, and all would be equally responsible for the hoax. No chance of indiscretion or belated qualms there. Their own interest ruled it out in each case.

And from the other men now involved there was as little danger of betrayal. Their gain would be vastly greater, but they had correspondingly more to lose. They would take every step required to insure their protection, and in doing that they would necessarily take the best of care of Phil Boles.

"How did you ever get such a thing smuggled in to Roye?" Phil asked. He'd swallowed half the drink Celia offered him at a gulp and now, a few minutes later, he was experiencing what might have been under different circumstances a comfortable glow, but which didn't entirely erase the awareness of having committed himself at this hour to an irrevocable line of action.

Celia stroked a fluffy lock of red-brown hair back from her forehead and glanced over at him. She had a narrow, pretty face, marred only by a suggestion of hardness about the mouth — which was a little more than ordinarily noticeable just now. Phil decided she felt something like his own tensions, for identical reasons. He was less certain about Major Wayne Jackson, a big, loose-jointed man with an easy-going smile and a pleasantly self-assured voice. The voice might be veering a trifle too far to the hearty side; but that was all.

"I didn't," Celia said. "It belonged to Frank. How he got it shipped in with him — or after him — from Earth I don't know. He never told me. When he died a couple of years ago, I took it over."

Phil gazed reflectively at the row of unfamiliar instruments covering half the table beside her. The "camera" which had taken an imprint of the Geest gun in Aunt Beulah's living room went with that equipment and had become an interior section of the largest of the instruments. "What do you call it?" he asked.

Celia looked irritated. Jackson laughed, said, "Why not tell him? Phil's feeling like we do — this is the last chance to look everything over, make sure nobody's slipped up, that nothing can go wrong. Right, Phil?"

Phil nodded. "Something like that."

Celia chewed her lip. "All right," she said. "It doesn't matter, I suppose — compared with the other." She tapped one of the instruments. "The set's called a duplicator. This one's around sixty years old. They're classified as a forgery device, and it's decidedly illegal for a private person to build one, own one, or use one."

"Why that?"

"Because forgery is ordinarily all they're good for. Frank was one of the best of the boys in that line before he found he'd been put on an outtransfer list."

Phil frowned. "But if it can duplicate any manufactured object —"

"It can. At an average expense around fifty times higher than it would take to make an ordinary reproduction without it. A duplicator's no use unless you want a reproduction that's absolutely indistinguishable from the model."

"I see." Phil was silent a moment. "After sixty years —"

"Don't worry, Phil," Jackson said. "It's in perfect working condition. We checked that on a number of samples."

"How do you know the copies were really indistinguishable?"

Celia said impatiently, "Because that's the way the thing works. When the Geest gun passed through the model plate, it was analyzed down to its last little molecule. The duplicate is now being built up from that analysis. Every fraction of every element used in the original will show up again exactly. Why do you think the stuff's so expensive?"

Phil grinned. "All right, I'm convinced. How do we get

rid of the inscription?"

"The gadget will handle that," Jackson said. "Crack that edge off, treat the cracked surface to match the wear of the rest." He smiled. "Makes an Earth forger's life look easy, doesn't it?"

"It is till they hook you," Celia said shortly. She finished her drink, set it on the table, added, "We've a few questions, too, Phil."

"The original gun," Jackson said. "Mind you, there's no slightest reason to expect an investigation. But after this starts rolling, our necks will be out just a little until we've got rid of that particular bit of incriminating evidence."

Phil pursed his lips. "I wouldn't worry about it. Nobody but Beulah ever looks at Uncle William's collection of oddities. Most of it's complete trash. And probably only she and you and I know there's a Geest gun among the things — William's cronies all passed away before he did. But if the gun disappeared now, Beulah would miss it. And that — since Earth government's made it illegal to possess Geest artifacts — *might* create attention."

Jackson fingered his chin thoughtfully, said, "Of course, there's always a way to make sure Beulah didn't kick up a fuss."

Phil hesitated. "Dr. Fitzsimmons gives Beulah another three months at the most," he said. "If she can stay out of the hospital for even the next eight weeks, he'll consider it some kind of miracle. That should be early enough to take care of the gun."

"It should be," Jackson said. "However, if there does happen to be an investigation before that time —"

Phil looked at him, said evenly, "We'd do whatever was necessary. It wouldn't be very agreeable, but my neck's out just as far as yours."

Celia laughed. "That's the reason we can all feel pretty safe," she observed. "Every last one of us is completely selfish — and there's no more dependable kind of person than that."

Jackson flushed a little, glanced at Phil, smiled. Phil shrugged. Major Wayne Jackson, native son, Fort Roye's second in command, was scheduled for the number one spot and a string of promotions via the transfer of the current commander, Colonel Thayer. Their Earthside associates would arrange for that as soon as the decision to turn Fort Roye into a Class A military base was reached. Phil himself could get by with the guaranteed retention of the CLU presidency, and a membership moving up year by year to the half million mark and beyond — he could get by very, very comfortably, in fact. While Celia Adams would develop a discreetly firm hold on every upcoming minor racket, facilitated by iron-clad protection and an enforced lack of all competitors.

"We're all thinking of Roye's future, Celia," Phil said amiably, "each in his own way. And the future looks pretty bright. In fact, the only possible stumbling block I can still see is right here on Roye, and it's Honest Silas Thayer. If our colonel covers up the Geest gun find tomorrow —"

Jackson grinned, shook his head. "Leave that to me, my boy — and to our very distinguished visitors from Earth. Commissioner Sanford has arranged to be in Thayer's company on Territorial Office business all day tomorrow. Science Officer Vaughn is dizzy with delight because Ronald Black and most of the newsgathering troop will inspect his diggings in the ruins in the morning, with the promise of giving his theories about the vanished natives of Roye a nice spread on Earth. Black will happen to ask me to accompany the party. Between Black and Sanford — and myself — Colonel Silas Thayer won't have a chance to suppress the discovery of a Geest gun on Roye until the military has had a chance to look into it fully. And the only one he can possibly blame for that will be Science Officer Norm Vaughn — for whom, I'll admit, I feel just a little bit sorry!"

First Lieutenant Norman Vaughn was an intense and frustrated young man whose unusually thick contact lenses and wide mouth gave him some resemblance to a melancholy frog. He suspected, correctly, that a good Science Officer would not have been transferred from Earth to Roye which was a planet deficient in scientific problems of any magnitude, and where requisitions for research purposes were infrequently and grudgingly granted.

The great spiraled ruin on the peninsula of Fort Roye had been Vaughn's one solace. Several similar deserted structures were known to be on the planet, but this was by far in the best condition and no doubt the most recently built. To him, if to no one else, it became clear that the construction had been carried out with conscious plan and purpose, and he gradually amassed great piles of notes to back up his theory that the vanished builders were of near-human intelligence. Unfortunately, their bodies appeared to have lacked hard and durable parts, since nothing that could be construed as their remains was found; and what Lieutenant Vaughn regarded as undeniable artifacts, on the level of very early Man's work, looked to others like chance shards and lumps of the tough, shell-like material of which the ruins were composed.

Therefore, while Vaughn was — as Jackson had pointed out — really dizzy with delight when Ronald Black, that giant of Earth's news media, first indicated an interest in the ruins and his theories about them, this feeling soon became mixed with acute anxiety. For such a chance surely would not come again if the visitors remained unconvinced by what he showed them, and what — actually — did he have to show? In the morning, when the party set out, Vaughn was in a noticeably nervous frame of mind.

Two hours later, he burst into the anteroom of the base commander's office in Fort Roye, where the warrant on duty almost failed to recognize him. Lieutenant Vaughn's eyes glittered through their thick lenses; his face was red and he was grinning from ear to ear. He pounded past the startled warrant, pulled open the door to the inner office where Colonel Thayer sat with the visiting Territorial Commissioner, and plunged inside.

"Sir," the warrant heard him quaver breathlessly, "I have the proof — the undeniable proof! They *were* intelligent beings. They did *not* die of disease. They were exterminated in war! They were . . . but see for yourself!" There was a thud as he dropped something on the polished table top between the commissioner and Colonel Thayer. "*That* was dug up just now — among their own artifacts!"

Silas Thayer was on his feet, sucking in his breath for the blast that would hurl his blundering Science Officer back out of the office. What halted him was an odd, choked exclamation from Commissioner Sanford. The colonel's gaze flicked over to the visitor, then followed Sanford's stare to the object on the table.

For an instant, Colonel Thayer froze.

Vaughn was bubbling on. "And, sir, I . . ."

"Shut up!" Thayer snapped. He continued immediately, "You say this was found in the diggings in the ruins?"

"Yes, sir — just now! It's . . ."

Lieutenant Vaughn checked himself under the colonel's

stare, some dawning comprehension of the enormous irregularities he'd committed showing in his flushed face. He licked his lips uncertainly.

"You will excuse me for a moment, sir," Thayer said to Commissioner Sanford. He picked the Geest gun up gingerly by its unmistakably curved shaft, took it over to the office safe, laid it inside and relocked the safe. He then left the office.

In an adjoining room, Thayer rapped out Major Wayne Jackson's code number on a communicator. He heard a faint click as Jackson's wrist speaker switched on, and said quickly, "Wayne, are you in a position to speak?"

"I am at the moment," Jackson's voice replied cautiously.

Colonel Thayer said, "Norm Vaughn just crashed in here with something he claims was found in the diggings. Sanford saw it, and obviously recognized it. We might be able to keep him quiet. But now some questions. Was that item actually dug up just now?"

"Apparently it was," Jackson said. "I didn't see it happen — I was talking to Black at the moment. But there are over a dozen witnesses who claim they did see it happen, including five or six of the news agency men."

"And they knew what it was?"

"Enough of them did."

Thayer cursed softly. "No chance that one of them pitched the thing into the diggings for an Earthside sensation?"

"I'm afraid not," Jackson said. "It was lying in the sifter after most of the sand and dust had been blown away."

"Why didn't you call me at once?"

"I've been holding down something like a mutiny here, Silas. Vaughn got away before I could stop him, but I grounded the other aircars till you could decide what to do. Our visitors don't like that. Neither do they like the fact that I've put a guard over the section where the find was made, and haven't let them talk to Norm's work crew.

"Ronald Black and his staff have been fairly reasonable, but there's been considerable mention of military high-handedness made by the others. This is the first moment I've been free."

"You did the right thing," Thayer said, "but I doubt it will help much now. Can you get hold of Ronald Black?"

"Yes, he's over there . . ."

"Colonel Thayer?" another voice inquired pleasantly a few seconds later.

"Mr. Black," the colonel said carefully, "what occurred in the diggings a short while ago may turn out to be a matter of great importance."

"That's quite obvious, sir."

"And that being the case," the colonel went on, "do you believe it would be possible to obtain a gentleman's agreement from all witnesses to make no mention of this apparent discovery until the information is released through the proper channels? I'm asking for your opinion."

"Colonel Thayer," Ronald Black's voice said, still pleasantly, "my opinion is that the only way you could keep the matter quiet is to arrest every civilian present, including myself, and hold us incommunicado. You have your duty, and we have ours. Ours does not include withholding information from the public which may signal the greatest shift in the conduct of the Geest War in the past two decades."

"I understand," Thayer said. He was silent for some seconds, and perhaps he, too, was gazing during that time at a

Fort Roye of the future — a Class A military base under his command, with Earth's great war vessels lined up along the length of the peninsula.

"Mr. Black," he said, "please be so good as to give your colleagues this word from me. I shall make the most thorough possible investigation of what has occurred and forward a prompt report, along with any material evidence obtained, to my superiors on Earth. None of you will receive any other statement from me or from anyone under my command. An attempt to obtain such a statement will, in fact, result in the arrest of the person or persons involved. Is that clear?"

"Quite clear, Colonel Thayer," Ronald Black said softly. "And entirely satisfactory."

"We have known for the past eight weeks," the man named Cranehart said, "that this was not what it appears to be . . . that is, a section of a Geest weapon."

He shoved the object in question across the desk towards Commissioner Sanford and Ronald Black. Neither of the two attempted to pick it up; they glanced at it, then returned their eyes attentively to Cranehart's face.

"It is, of course, an excellent copy," Cranehart went on, "produced with a professional forger's equipment. As I imagine you're aware, that should have made it impossible to distinguish from the original weapon. However . . . there's no real harm in telling you this now . . . Geest technology has taken somewhat different turns than our own. In their weapons they employ traces of certain elements which we are only beginning to learn to maintain in stable form. That is a matter your government has kept from public knowledge because we don't wish the Geests to learn from human prisoners how much information we are gaining from them.

"The instrument which made this copy naturally did not have such elements at its disposal. So it employed their lower homologues and in that manner successfully produced an almost identical model. In fact, the only significant difference is that such a gun, if it had been a complete model, could not possibly have been fired." He smiled briefly. "But that, I think you will agree, *is* a significant difference! We knew as soon as the so-called Geest gun was examined that it could only have been made by human beings."

"Then," Commissioner Sanford said soberly, "its apparent discovery on Roye during our visit was a deliberate hoax —"

Cranehart nodded. "Of course."

Ronald Black said, "I fail to see why you've kept this quiet. You needn't have given away any secrets. Meanwhile the wave of public criticism at the government's seeming hesitancy to take action on the discovery — that is, to rush protection to the threatened Territorial Segments — has reached almost alarming proportions. You could have stopped it before it began two months ago with a single announcement."

"Well, yes," Cranehart said. "There were other considerations. Incidentally, Mr. Black, we are not unappreciative of the fact that the news media under your own control exercised a generous restraint in the matter."

"For which," Black said dryly, "I am now very thankful."

"As for the others," Cranehart went on, "the government has survived periods of criticism before. That is not important. The important thing is that the Geest War has been with us for more than a human life span now . . . and it becomes difficult for many to bear in mind that until its conclusion no acts that might reduce our ability to prosecute it can be tolerated."

Ronald Black said slowly, "So you've been delaying the announcement until you could find out who was responsible for the hoax."

"We were interested," Cranehart said, "only in the important men — the dangerous men. We don't care much who else is guilty of what. This, you see, is a matter of expediency, not of justice." He looked for a moment at the politely questioning, somewhat puzzled faces across the desk, went on, "When you leave this room, each of you will be conducted to an office where you will be given certain papers to sign. That is the first step."

There was silence for some seconds. Ronald Black took a cigarette from a platinum case, tapped it gently on the desk, put it to his mouth and lit it. Cranehart went on, "It would have been impossible to unravel this particular conspiracy if the forgery had been immediately exposed. At that time, no one had taken any obvious action. Then, within a few days — with the discovery apparently confirmed by our silence — normal maneuverings in industry and finance were observed to be under way. If a major shift in war policy was pending, if one or more key bases were to be established in Territorial Segments previously considered beyond the range of Geest reconnaissance and therefore secure from attack, this would be to somebody's benefit on Earth."

"Isn't it always?" Black murmured.

"Of course. It's a normal procedure, ordinarily of no concern to government. It can be predicted with considerable accuracy to what group or groups the ultimate advantage in such a situation will go. But in these past weeks, it became apparent that somebody else was winning out . . . somebody who could have won out only on the basis of careful and extensive preparation for this very situation.

"That was abnormal, and it was the appearance of an abnormal pattern for which we had been waiting. We find there are seven men involved. These men will be deprived of the advantage they have gained."

Ronald Black shook his head, said, "You're making a mistake, Cranehart. I'm signing no papers."

"Nor I," Sanford said thickly.

Cranehart rubbed the side of his nose with a fingertip, said meditatively, "You won't be forced to. Not directly." He nodded at the window. "On the landing flange out there is an aircar. It is possible that this aircar will be found wrecked in the mountains some four hundred miles north of here early tomorrow morning. Naturally, we have a satisfactory story prepared to cover such an eventuality."

Sanford whitened slowly. He said, "So you'd resort to murder!"

Cranehart was silent for a few seconds. "Mr. Sanford," he said then, "you, as a member of the Territorial Office, know very well that the Geest War has consumed over four hundred million human lives to date. That is the circumstance which obliges your government to insist on your co-operation. I advise you to give it."

"But you have no proof! You have nothing but surmises —"

"Consider this," Cranehart said. "A conspiracy of the type I have described constitutes a capital offense under present conditions. Are you certain that you would prefer us to continue to look for proof?"

Ronald Black said in a harsh voice, "And what would the outcome be if we did choose to co-operate?"

"Well, we can't afford to leave men of your type in a position of influence, Mr. Black," Cranehart said amiably. "And you understand, I'm sure, that it would be entirely too difficult to keep you under proper surveillance on Earth —"

Celia Adams said from outside the cabin door, "I think it is them, Phil. Both cars have started to circle."

Phil Boles came to the door behind her and looked up. It was early evening — Roye's sun just down, and a few stars out. The sky above the sea was still light. After a moment, he made out the two aircars moving in a wide, slow arc far overhead. He glanced at his watch.

"Twenty minutes late," he remarked. "But it couldn't be anyone else. And if they hadn't all come along, they wouldn't have needed two cars." He hesitated. "We can't tell how they're going to take this, Celia, but they may have decided already that they could make out better without us." He nodded towards the edge of the cliff. "Short way over there, and a long drop to the water! So don't let them surprise you."

She said coldly, "I won't. And I've used guns before this."

"Wouldn't doubt it." Phil reached back behind the door, picked up a flarelight standing beside a heavy machine rifle, and came outside. He pointed the light at the cars and touched the flash button briefly three times. After a moment, there were two answering flashes from the leading car.

"So Wayne Jackson's in the front car," Phil said. "Now let's see what they do." He returned the light to its place behind the door and came out again, standing about twelve feet to one side of Celia. The aircars vanished inland, came back at treetop level a few minutes later. One settled down quietly between the cabin and the edge of the cliff, the other following but dropping to the ground a hundred yards away, where it stopped. Phil glanced over at Celia, said softly, "Watch that one!" She nodded almost imperceptibly, right hand buried in her jacket pocket.

The near door of the car before them opened. Major Wayne Jackson, hatless and in hunting clothes, climbed out, staring at them. He said, "Anyone else here?"

"Just Celia and myself," Phil said.

Jackson turned, spoke into the car and two men, similarly dressed, came out behind him. Phil recognized Ronald Black and Sanford. The three started over to the cabin, stopped a dozen feet away.

Jackson said sardonically, "Our five other previous Earthside partners are in the second car. In spite of your insistence to meet the whole group, they don't want you and Celia to see their faces. They don't wish to be identifiable." He touched his coat lapel. "They'll hear what we're saying over this communicator and they could talk to you, but won't unless they feel it's necessary. You'll have to take my word for it that we're all present."

"That's good enough," Phil said.

"All right," Jackson went on, "now what did you mean by forcing us to take this chance? Let me make it plain. Colonel Thayer hasn't been accused of collaborating in the Roye gun hoax, but he got a black eye out of the affair just the same. And don't forget that a planet with colonial status is technically under martial law, which includes the civilians. If Silas Thayer can get his hands on the guilty persons, the situation will become a lot more unpleasant than it already is."

Phil addressed Ronald Black, "Then how about you two? When you showed up here again on a transfer list, Thayer must have guessed why."

Black shook his head. "Both of us exercised the privilege of changing our names just prior to the outtransfer. He doesn't know we're on Roye. We don't intend to let him find out."

Phil asked, "Did you make any arrangements to get out of Roye again?"

"Before leaving Earth?" Black showed his teeth in a humorless smile. "Boles, you have no idea of how abruptly and completely the government men cut us off from our every resource! We were given no opportunity to draw up plans to escape from exile, believe me."

Phil glanced over at Celia. "In that case," he said, a little thickly, "we'd better see if we can't draw some up together immediately."

Jackson asked, staring, "What are you talking about, Phil? Don't think for a moment Silas Thayer isn't doing what he can to find out who put that trick over on him. I'm not at all sure he doesn't suspect me. And if he can tie it to us, it's our neck. If you have some crazy idea of getting off the planet now, let me tell you that for the next few years we can't risk making a single move! If we stay quiet, we're safe. We —"

"I don't think we'd be safe," Phil said.

On his right, Celia Adams added sharply, "The gentleman in the other car who's just started to lower that window had better raise it again! If he's got good eyesight, he'll see I have a gun pointed at him. Yes, that's much better! Go on, Phil."

"Have you both gone out of your minds?" Jackson demanded.

"No," Celia said. She laughed with a sudden shakiness in her tone, added, "Though I don't know why we haven't! We've thought of the possibility that the rest of you might feel it would be better if Phil and I weren't around any more, Wayne."

"That's nonsense!" Jackson said.

"Maybe. Anyway, don't try it. You wouldn't be doing yourselves a favor even if it worked. Better listen now."

"Listen to what?" Jackson demanded exasperatedly. "I'm telling you it will be all right, if we just don't make any mistakes. The only real pieces of evidence were your duplicator and the original gun. Since we're rid of those —"

"We're not rid of the gun, Wayne," Phil said. "I still have it. I haven't dared get rid of it."

"You . . . what do you mean?"

"I was with Beulah in the Fort Roye hospital when she died," Phil said. He added to Ronald Black, "That was two days after the ship brought the seven of you in."

Black nodded, his eyes alert. "Major Jackson informed me."

"She was very weak, of course, but quite lucid," Phil went on. "She talked a good deal — reminiscing, and in a rather happy vein. She finally mentioned the Geest gun, and how Uncle William used to keep us boys . . . Wayne and me . . . spell-bound with stories about the Gunderland Battle, and how he'd picked the gun up there."

Jackson began, "And what does —"

"He didn't get the gun there," Phil said. "Beulah said Uncle William came in from Earth with the first shipment of settlers and was never off Roye again in his life."

"He . . . then —"

Phil said, "Don't you get it? He found the gun right here on Roye. Beulah thought it was awfully funny. William was an old fool, she said, but the best liar she'd ever known. He came in with the thing one day after he'd been traipsing around the back country, and said it looked 'sort of' like pictures of Geest guns he'd seen, and that he was going to put the inscription on it and have some fun now and then." Phil took a deep breath. "Uncle William found it lying in a pile of ashes where someone had made camp a few days before. He figured it would have been a planetary speedster some rich sportsmen from Earth had brought in for a taste of outworld hunting on Roye, and that one of them had dumped the broken oddball gun into the fire to get rid of it.

"That was thirty-six years ago. Beulah remembered it happened a year before I was born."

There was silence for some seconds. Then Ronald Black said evenly, "And what do you conclude, Boles?"

Phil looked at him. "I'd conclude that Norm Vaughn was right about there having been some fairly intelligent creatures here once. The Geests ran into them and exterminated them as they usually do. That might have been a couple of centuries back. Then, thirty-six years ago, one of their scouts slipped in here without being spotted, found human beings on the planet, looked around a little and left again."

He took the Geest gun from his pocket, hefted it in his hand. "We have the evidence here," he said. "We had it all the time and didn't know it."

Ronald Black said dryly, "We may have the evidence. But we have no slightest proof at all now that that's what it is."

"I know it," Phil said. "Now Beulah's gone . . . well, we couldn't even prove that William Boles never left the planet, for that matter. There weren't any records to speak of being kept in the early days." He was silent a moment. "Supposing," he said, "we went ahead anyway. We hand the gun in, with the story I just told you —"

Jackson made a harsh, laughing sound. "That would hang us fast, Phil!"

"And nothing else?"

"Nothing else," Black said with finality. "Why should

anyone believe the story now? There are a hundred more likely ways in which a Geest gun could have got to Roye. The gun is tangible evidence of the hoax, but that's all."

Phil asked, "Does anybody . . . including the cautious gentlemen in the car over there . . . disagree with that?"

There was silence again. Phil shrugged, turned towards the cliff edge, drew his arm back and hurled the Geest gun far up and out above the sea. Still without speaking, the others turned their heads to watch it fall towards the water, then looked back at him.

"I didn't think very much of that possibility myself," Phil said unsteadily. "But one of you might have. All right — *we* know the Geests know we're here. But we won't be able to convince anyone else of it. And, these last few years, the war seems to have been slowing down again. In the past, that's always meant the Geests were preparing a big new surprise operation.

"So the other thing now — the business of getting off Roye. It can't be done unless some of you have made prior arrangements for it Earthside. If it had been possible in any other way, I'd have been out of this place ten years ago."

Ronald Black said carefully, "Very unfortunately, Boles, no such arrangements have been made."

"Then there it is," Phil said. "I suppose you see now why I thought this group should get together. The ten master-minds! Well, we've hoaxed ourselves into a massive jam. Now let's find out if there's any possible way — *any possibility at all!* — of getting out of it again."

A voice spoke tinnily from Jackson's lapel communicator. "Major Jackson?"

"Yes?" Jackson said.

"Please persuade Miss Adams that it is no longer necessary to point her gun at this car. In view of the stated emergency, we feel we had better come out now — and join the conference."

FROM THE RECORDS OF
THE TERRITORIAL OFFICE, 2345 A.D.

. . . It is generally acknowledged that the Campaign of the 132nd Segment marked the turning point of the Geest War. Following the retransfer of Colonel Silas Thayer to Earth, the inspired leadership of Major Wayne Jackson and his indefatigable and exceptionally able assistants, notably CLU President Boles, transformed the technically unfortified and thinly settled key world of Roye within twelve years into a virtual death trap for any invading force. Almost half of the Geest fleet which eventually arrived there was destroyed in the first week subsequent to the landing, and few of the remaining ships were sufficiently undamaged to be able to lift again. The enemy relief fleet, comprising an estimated forty per cent of the surviving Geest space power, was intercepted in the 134th Segment by the combined Earth forces under Admiral McKenna's command and virtually annihilated.

In the following two years . . .

THE WINDS OF TIME

Gefty Rammer came along the narrow passages between the *Silver Queen's* control compartment and the staterooms, trying to exchange the haggard look on his face for one of competent self-assurance. There was nothing to gain by letting his two passengers suspect that during the past few minutes their pilot, the owner of Rammer Spacelines, had been a bare step away from plain and fancy gibbering.

He opened the door to Mr. Maulbow's stateroom and went inside. Mr. Maulbow, face very pale, eyes closed, lay on his back on the couch, still unconscious. He'd been knocked out when some unknown forces suddenly started batting the *Silver Queen's* turnip-shape around as the *Queen* had never been batted before in her eighteen years of space-faring. Kerim Ruse, Maulbow's secretary, knelt beside her employer, checking his pulse. She looked anxiously up at Gefty.

"What did you find out?" she asked in a voice that was not very steady.

Gefty shrugged. "Nothing definite as yet. The ship hasn't been damaged — she's a tough tub. That's one good point. Otherwise . . . well, I climbed into a suit and took a look out the escape hatch. And I saw the same thing there that the screens show. Whatever that is."

"You've no idea then of what's happened to us, or where we are?" Miss Ruse persisted. She was a rather small girl with large, beautiful gray eyes and thick blue-black hair. At the moment, she was barefoot and in a sleeping outfit which consisted of something soft wrapped around her top, soft and floppy trousers below. The black hair was tousled and she looked around fifteen. She'd been asleep in her stateroom when something smacked the *Queen*, and she was sensible enough then not to climb out of the bunk's safety field until the ship finally stopped shuddering and bucking about. That made her the only one of the three persons aboard who had collected no bruises. She was scared, of course, but taking the situation very well.

Gefty said carefully, "There're a number of possibilities. It's obvious that the *Queen* has been knocked out of normspace, and it may take some time to find out how to get her back there. But the main thing is that the ship's intact. So far, it doesn't look too bad."

Miss Ruse seemed somewhat reassured. Gefty could hardly have said the same for himself. He was a qualified normspace and subspace pilot. He had put in a hitch with the Federation Navy, and for the past eight years he'd been ferrying his own two ships about the Hub and not infrequently beyond the Federation's space territories, but he had never heard of a situation like this. What he saw in the viewscreens when the ship steadied enough to let him pick himself off the instrument room floor, and again, a few minutes later and with much more immediacy, from the escape hatch, made no sense — seemed simply to have no meaning. The pressure meters said there was a vacuum outside the *Queen's* skin. That vacuum was dark, even pitch-black but here and there came momentary suggestions of vague light and color. Occasional pinpricks of brightness showed and were gone. And there had been one startling phenomenon like a distant, giant explosion, a sudden pallid glare in the dark, which appeared far ahead of the *Queen* and, for the instant it remained in sight, seemed to be rushing directly towards them. It had given Gefty the feeling that the ship itself was plowing at high speed through this eerie medium. But he had cut the *Queen's* drives to the merest idling pulse as soon as he staggered back to the control console and got his first look at the screens, so it must have been the light that had moved.

But such details were best not discussed with a passenger. Kerim Ruse would be arriving at enough disquieting speculations on her own; the less he told her, the better. There was the matter of the ship's location instruments. The only set Gefty had been able to obtain any reading on were the direction indicators. And what they appeared to indicate was that the *Silver Queen* was turning on a new heading something like twenty times a second.

Gefty asked, "Has Mr. Maulbow shown any signs of waking up?"

Kerim shook her head. "His breathing and pulse seem all right, and that bump on his head doesn't look really bad, but he hasn't moved at all. Can you think of anything else we might do for him, Gefty?"

"Not at the moment," Gefty said. "He hasn't broken any bones. We'll see how he feels when he comes out of it." He was wondering about Mr. Maulbow and the fact that this charter had showed some unusual features from the beginning.

Kerim was a friendly sort of girl; they'd got to calling each other by their first names within a day or two after the trip started. But after that, she seemed to be avoiding him; and Gefty guessed that Maulbow had spoken to her, probably to make sure that Kerim didn't let any of her employer's secrets slip out.

Maulbow himself was as aloof and taciturn a client as Rammer Spacelines ever had picked up. A lean, blond character of indeterminate age, with pale eyes, hard mouth. Why he had selected a bulky semifreighter like the *Queen* for a mineralogical survey jaunt to a lifeless little sun system far beyond the outposts of civilization was a point he didn't discuss. Gefty, needing the charter money, had restrained his curiosity. If Maulbow wanted only a pilot and preferred to do all the rest of the work himself, that was certainly Maulbow's affair. And if he happened to be up to something illegal — though it was difficult to imagine what — Customs would nail him when they got back to the Hub.

But those facts looked a little different now.

Gefty scratched his chin, inquired, "Do you happen to know where Mr. Maulbow keeps the keys to the storage vault?"

Kerim looked startled. "Why, no! I couldn't permit you to take the keys anyway while he . . . while he's unconscious! You know that."

Gefty grunted. "Any idea of what he has locked up in the vault?"

"You shouldn't ask me — " Her eyes widened. "Why, that couldn't possibly have anything to do with what's happened!"

He might, Gefty thought, have reassured her a little too much. He said, "I wouldn't know. But I don't want to just sit here and wonder about it until Maulbow wakes up. Until we're back in normspace, we'd better not miss any bets. Because one thing's sure — if this has happened to anybody else, they didn't turn up again to report it. You see?"

Kerim apparently did. She went pale, then said hesitantly, "Well . . . the sealed cases Mr. Maulbow brought out from the Hub with him had some very expensive instruments in them. That's all I know. He's always trusted me not to pry into his business any more than my secretarial duties required, and of course I haven't."

"You don't know then what it was he brought up from

that moon a few hours ago — those two big cases he stowed away in the vault?"

"No, I don't, Gefty. You see, he hasn't told me what the purpose of this trip is. I only know that it's a matter of great importance to him." Kerim paused, added, "From the careful manner Mr. Maulbow handled the cases with the cranes, I had the impression that whatever was inside them must be quite heavy."

"I noticed that," Gefty said. It wasn't much help. "Well, I'll tell *you* something now," he went on. "I let your boss keep both sets of keys to the storage vault because he insisted on it when he signed the charter. What I didn't tell him was that I could make up a duplicate set any time in around half an hour."

"Oh! Have you — ?"

"Not yet. But I intend to take a look at what Mr. Maulbow's got in that vault now, with or without his consent. You'd better run along and get dressed while I take him up to the instrument room."

"Why move him?" Kerim asked.

"The instrument room's got an overall safety field. I've turned it on now, and if something starts banging us around again, the room will be the safest place on the ship. I'll bring his personal luggage up too, and you can start looking through it for the keys. You may find them before I get a new set made. Or he may wake up and tell us where they are."

Kerim Ruse gave her employer a dubious glance, then nodded, said, "I imagine you're right, Gefty," and pattered hurriedly out of the stateroom. A few minutes later, she arrived, fully dressed, in the instrument room. Gefty looked around from the table-shelf where he had laid out his tools, and said, "He hasn't stirred. His suitcases are over there. I've unlocked them."

Kerim gazed at what showed in the screens about the control console and shivered slightly. She said, "I was thinking, Gefty . . . isn't there something they call Space Three?"

"Sure. Pseudospace. But that isn't where we are. There're some special-built Navy tubs that can operate in that stuff if they don't stay too long. A ship like the *Queen* . . . well, you and I and everything else in here would be frozen solid by now if we'd got sucked somehow into Space Three."

"I see," Kerim said uncomfortably. Gefty heard her move over to the suitcases. After a moment, she asked, "What do the vault keys look like?"

"You can't miss them if he's just thrown them in there. They're over six inches long. What kind of a guy is this Maulbow? A scientist?"

"I couldn't say, Gefty. He's never referred to himself as a scientist. I've had this job a year and a half. Mr. Maulbow is a very considerate employer . . . one of the nicest men I've known, really. But it was simply understood that I should ask no questions about the business beyond what I actually needed to know for my work."

"What's the business called?"

"Maulbow Engineering."

"Big help," Gefty observed, somewhat sourly. "Those instruments he brought along . . . he build those himself?"

"No, but I think he designed some of them — probably most of them. The companies he had doing the actual work appeared to have a terrible time getting everything exactly the way Mr. Maulbow wanted it — There's nothing that looks like a set of keys in those first two suitcases, Gefty."

"Well," Gefty said, "if you don't find them in the others, you might start thumping around to see if he's got secret compartments in his luggage somewhere."

"I do wish," Kerim Ruse said uneasily, "that Mr. Maulbow would regain consciousness. It seems so . . . so under-handed to be doing these things behind his back!"

Gefty grunted noncommittally. He wasn't at all certain by now that he wanted his secretive client to wake up before he'd checked on the contents of the *Queen's* storage vault.

Fifteen minutes later, Gefty Rammer was climbing down to the storage deck in the *Queen's* broad stern, the newly fashioned set of vault keys clanking heavily in his coat pocket. Kerim had remained with her employer who was getting back his color but still hadn't opened his eyes. She hadn't found the original keys. Gefty wasn't sure she'd tried too hard, though she seemed to realize the seriousness of the situation now. But her loyalty to Mr. Maulbow could make no further difference, and she probably felt more comfortable for it.

Lights went on automatically in the wide passage lead-ing from the cargo lock to the vault as Gefty turned into it. His steps echoed between the steel bulkheads on either side. He paused a moment before the big circular vault doors, lis-tening to the purr of the *Queen's* idling engines in the next compartment. The familiar sound was somehow reassur-ing. He inserted the first key, turned it over twice, drew it out again and pressed one of the buttons in the control panel beside the door. The heavy slab of steel moved side-ways with a soft, hissing sound, vanished into the wall. Gefty slid the other key into the lock of the inner door. A few sec-onds later, the vault entrance lay open before him.

He stood still again, wrinkling his nose. The area ahead was only dimly illuminated — the shaking-up the *Queen* had undergone had disturbed the lighting system here. And what was that odor? Rather sharp, unpleasant; it might have been spilled ammonia. Gefty stepped through the door into the wide, short entrance passage beyond it, turned to the right and peered about in the semidarkness of the vault.

Two great steel cases — the ones Maulbow had taken down to an airless moon surface, loaded up with something and brought back to the *Queen* — were jammed awkwardly into a corner, in a manner which suggested they'd slid into it when the ship was being knocked around. One of them was open and appeared to be empty. Gefty wasn't sure of the other. In the dimness beside them lay the loose coils of some very thick, dark cable — And standing near the center of the floor was a thing that at once riveted his attention on it completely. He sucked his breath in softly, feeling chilled.

He realized he hadn't really believed his own hunch. But, of course, if it hadn't been an unheard-of outside force that plucked the *Queen* out of normspace and threw her into this elsewhere, then it must be something Maulbow had put on board. And that something had to be a machine of some kind —

It was.

About it he could make out a thin gleaming of wires — a jury-rigged safety field. Within the flimsy-looking protective cage was a double bank of instruments, some of them alive with the flicker and glow of lights. Those must be the very expensive and difficult-to-build items Maulbow had brought out from the Hub. Beside them stood the machine, squat and ponderous. In the vague light, it looked misshaped and discolored. A piece of equipment that had taken a bad beating of some kind. But it was functioning. As he stared, intermittent bursts of clicking noises rose from it, like the staccato of irregular gunfire.

For a moment, questions raced in disorder through his mind. What was it? Why had it been on that moon? Part of another ship, wrecked now . . . a ship that had been at home *here*? Was it some sort of drive?

Maulbow must know. He'd known enough to design the instruments required to bring the battered monster back to life. On the other hand, he had not foreseen in all detail what could happen once the thing was in operation, because the *Queen's* sudden buck-jumping act had surprised him and knocked him out.

The first step, in any event, was to get Maulbow awake now. To tamper with a device like this, before learning as much as one could about it, would be lunatic foolhardiness. It looked like too good a bet that the next serious mistake made by anybody would finish them all —

Perhaps it was only because Gefty's nerves were on edge that he grew aware at that point in his reflections of two minor signals from his senses. One was that the smell of ammonia, which he had almost stopped noticing, was becoming appreciably stronger. The other was the faintest of sounds — a whispering suggestion of motion somewhere behind him. But here in the storage vault nothing should have moved, and Gefty's muscles were tensing as his head came around. Almost in the same instant, he flung himself wildly to one side, stumbling and regaining his balance as something big and dark slapped heavily down on the floor at the point where he had stood. Then he was darting up through the entrance passage, turning, and knocking down the lock switches on the outside door panel.

It came flowing around the corner of the passage behind him as the vault doors began to slide together. He was aware mainly of swift, smooth, oiling motion like that of a big snake; then, for a fraction of a second, a strip of brighter light from the outside passage showed a long, heavy wedge of a head, a green metal-glint of staring eyes.

The doors closed silently into their frames and locked. The thing was inside. But it was almost a minute then before Gefty could control his shaking legs enough to start moving back towards the main deck. In the half-dark of the vault, it had looked like a big coiled cable lying next to the packing cases. Like Maulbow, it might have been battered around and knocked out during the recent disturbance; and when it recovered, it had found Gefty in the vault with it. But it might also have been awake all the while, waiting cunningly until Gefty's attention seemed fixed elsewhere before launching its attack. It was big enough to have flattened him and smashed every bone in his body if the stroke had landed.

Some kind of guard animal — a snakelike watchdog? What other connection could it have with the mystery machine? Perhaps Maulbow had intended to leave it confined in one of the cases, and it had broken loose —

Too many questions by now, Gefty thought. But Maulbow had the answers.

He was hurrying up the main deck's central passage when Maulbow's voice addressed him sharply from a door he'd just passed.

"Stop right there, Rammer! Don't dare to move! I —"

The voice ended on a note of surprise. Gefty's reaction had not been too rational, but it was prompt. Maulbow's tone and phrasing implied he was armed. Gefty wasn't, but he kept a gun in the instrument room for emergencies. He'd been through a whole series of unnerving experiences, winding up with being shagged out of his storage vault by something that stank of ammonia and looked like a giant snake. To have one of the *Queen's* passengers order him to stand where he was topped it off. Every other consideration was swept aside by a great urge to get his hands on his gun.

He glanced back, saw Maulbow coming out of the half-opened door, something like a twenty-inch, thin, white rod in one hand. Then Gefty went bounding on along the passage, hunched forward and zigzagging from wall to wall to give Maulbow — if the thing he held was a weapon and he actually intended to use it — as small and erratic a target as possible. Maulbow shouted angrily behind him. Then, as Gefty came up to the next cross-passage, a line of white fire seared through the air across his shoulders and smashed off the passage wall.

With that, he was around the corner, and boiling mad. He had no great liking for gunfire, but it didn't shake him like the silently attacking beast in the dark storage had done. He reached the deserted instrument room not many seconds later, had his gun out and cocked, and was faced back towards the passage by which he had entered. Maulbow, if he had pursued without hesitation, should be arriving by now. But the passage stayed quiet. Gefty couldn't see into it from where he stood. He waited, trying to steady his breathing, wondering where Kerim Ruse was and what had got into Maulbow. After a moment, without taking his eyes from the passage entrance, he reached into the wall closet from which he had taken the gun and fished out another souvenir of his active service days, a thin-bladed knife in a slip-sheath. Gefty worked the fastenings of the sheath over his left wrist and up his forearm under his coat, tested the release to make sure it was functioning, and shook his coat sleeve back into place.

The passage was still quiet. Gefty moved softly over to one of the chairs, took a small cushion from it and pitched it out in front of the entrance.

There was a hiss. The cushion turned in midair into a puff of bright white fire. Gefty aimed his gun high at the far passage wall just beyond the entrance and pulled the trigger. It was a projectile gun. He heard the slug screech off the slick plastic bulkhead and go slamming down the passage. Somebody out there made a startled, incoherent noise. But not the kind of a noise a man makes when he's just been hit.

"If you come in here armed," Gefty called, "I'll blow your head off. Want to stop this nonsense now?"

There was a moment's silence. Then Maulbow's voice replied shakily from the passage. He seemed to be standing about twenty feet back from the room.

"If you'll end your thoughtless attempts at interference, Rammer," he said, "there will be no trouble." He was speaking with the restraint of a man who is in a state of cold fury. "You're endangering us all. You must realize that you have no understanding of what you are doing."

Well, the last could be true enough. "We'll talk about it," Gefty said without friendliness. "I haven't done anything yet, but I'm not just handing the ship over to you. And what have you done with Miss Ruse?"

Maulbow hesitated again. "She's in the map room," he said then. "I . . . it was necessary to restrict her movements for a while. But you might as well let her out now. We must reach an agreement without loss of time."

Gefty glanced over his shoulder at the small closed door of the map room. There was no lock on the door, and he had heard no sound from inside; this might be some trick. But it wouldn't take long to find out. He backed up to the wall, pushed the door open and looked inside.

Kerim was there, sitting on a chair in one corner of the tiny room. The reason she hadn't made any noise became clear. She and the chair were covered by a rather closely fitting sack of transparent, glistening fabric. She stared out through it despairingly at Gefty, her lips moving urgently. But no sound came from the sack.

Gefty called angrily, "Maulbow —"

"Don't excite yourself, Rammer." There was a suggestion of what might be contempt in Maulbow's tone now. "The girl hasn't been harmed. She can breathe easily through the restrainer. And you can remove it by pulling at the material from outside."

Gefty's mouth tightened. "I'll keep my gun on the passage while I do it —"

Maulbow didn't answer. Gefty edged back into the map room, tentatively grasped the transparent stuff above Kerim's shoulder. To his surprise, it parted like wet tissue. He pulled sharply, and in a moment Kerim came peeling herself out of it, her face tear-stained, working desperately with hands, elbows and shoulders.

"Gefty," she gasped, "he . . . Mr. Maulbow —"

"He's out in the passage there," Gefty said. "He can hear you." His glance shifted for an instant to the wall where a second of the shroudlike transparencies was hanging. And who could that have been intended for, he thought, but Gefty Rammer? He added, "We've had a little trouble."

"Oh!" She looked out of the room towards the passage, then at the gun in Gefty's hand, then up at his face.

"Maulbow," Gefty went on, speaking distinctly enough to make sure Maulbow heard, "has a gun, too. He'll stay there in the passage and we'll stay in the instrument room until we agree on what should be done. He's responsible for what's happened and seems to know where we are."

He looked at Kerim's frightened eyes, dropped his voice to a whisper. "Don't let this worry you too much. I haven't found out just what he's up to, but so far his tricks have pretty much backfired. He was counting on taking us both by surprise, for one thing. That didn't work, so now he'd like us to co-operate."

"Are you going to?"

Gefty shrugged. "Depends on what he has in mind. I'm just interested in getting us out of this alive. Let's hear what Maulbow has to say —"

Some minutes later Gefty was trying to decide whether it was taking a worse risk to believe what Maulbow said than to keep things stalled on the chance that he was lying.

Kerim Ruse, perched stiffly erect on the edge of a chair, eyes big and round, face almost colorless, apparently believed Maulbow and was wishing she didn't. There was, of course, some supporting evidence . . . primarily the improbable appearance of their surroundings. The pencil-thin fire-spouter and the sleazy-looking "restrainer" had a sufficiently unfamiliar air to go with Maulbow's story; but as far as Gefty knew, either of them could have been manufactured in the Hub.

Then there was the janandra — the big, snakish thing in the storage which Maulbow had brought back up from the moon along with the battered machine. It had been, he said, his shipboard companion on another voyage. It wasn't ordinarily aggressive — Gefty's sudden appearance in the vault must have startled it into making an attack. It was not exactly a pet. There was a psychological relationship between it and Maulbow which Maulbow would not attempt to explain because Gefty and Kerim would be unable to grasp its significance. The janandra was essential, in this unexplained manner, to his well-being.

That item was almost curious enough to seem to substantiate his other statements; but it didn't really prove anything. The only point Gefty didn't question in the least was that they were in a bad spot which might be getting worse rapidly. His gaze shifted back to the screens. What he saw out there, surrounding the ship, was, according to Maulbow, an illusion of space created by the time flow in which they were moving.

Also according to Maulbow, there was a race of the future, human in appearance, with machines to sail the current of time through the universe — to run and tack with the winds of time, dipping in and out of the normspace of distant periods and galaxies as they chose. Maulbow, one of the explorers, had met disaster a million light-years from the home of his kind, centuries behind them, his vehicle wrecked on an airless moon with damaged control unit and shattered instruments. He had made his way to a human civilization to obtain the equipment he needed, and returned at last with the *Silver Queen* to where the time-sailer lay buried.

Gefty's lip curled. No, he wasn't buying all that just yet — but if Maulbow was *not* lying, then the unseen stars were racing past, the mass of the galaxy beginning to slide by, eventually to be lost forever beyond a black distance no space drive could span. The matter simply had to be settled quickly. But Maulbow was also strained and impatient, and if his impatience could be increased a little more, he might start telling the things that really mattered, the things Gefty had to know. Gefty asked slowly, as if hesitant to commit himself, "Why did you bring us along?"

The voice from the passage snapped, "Because my resources were nearly exhausted, Rammer! I couldn't obtain a new ship. Therefore I chartered yours; and you came with it. As for Miss Ruse — in spite of every precaution, my activities may have aroused suspicion and curiosity among your people. When I disappeared, Miss Ruse might have been questioned. I couldn't risk being followed to the wreck of the sailer, so I took her with me. And what does that mean against what I have offered you? The greatest adventure — followed, I give you my solemn word, by a safe return to your own place and time, and the most generous compensations for any inconvenience you may have suffered!"

Kerim, looking up at Gefty, shook her head violently. Gefty said, "We find it difficult to take you on trust now, Maulbow. Why do you want to get into the instrument room?"

Maulbow was silent for some seconds. Then he said, "As I told you, this ship would not have been buffeted about during the moments of transfer if the control unit were operating with complete efficiency. Certain adjustments will have to be made in the unit, and this should be done promptly."

"Where do the ship instruments come in?" Gefty asked.

"I can determine the nature of the problem from them. When I was ... stranded ... the unit was seriously damaged. My recent repairs were necessarily hasty. I —"

"What caused the crack-up?"

Maulbow said, tone taut with impatience, "Certain sections of the Great Current are infested with dangerous forces. I shall not attempt to describe them . . ."

"I wouldn't get it?"

"I don't pretend to understand them very well myself, Rammer. They are not life but show characteristics of life — even of intelligent life. If you can imagine radiant energy being capable of conscious hostility. . . ."

There was a chill at the back of Gefty's neck. "A big, fast-moving light?"

"Yes!" Sharp concern showed suddenly in the voice from the passage. "You . . . when did you see that?"

Gefty glanced at the screens. "Twice since you've been talking. And once before — immediately after we got tumbled around."

"Then we can waste no more time, Rammer. Those forces are sensitive to the fluctuations of the control unit. If they were close enough to be seen, they're aware the ship is here. They were attempting to locate it."

"What could they do?"

Maulbow said, "A single attack was enough to put the control unit out of operation in my sailer. The Great Current then rejected us instantly. A ship of this size might afford more protection, which is the reason I chose it. But if the control unit is not adjusted immediately to enable it to take us out of this section, the attacks will continue until the ship — and we — have been destroyed."

Gefty drew a deep breath. "There's another solution to that problem, Maulbow. Miss Ruse and I prefer it. And if you meant what you said — that you'd see to it we got back eventually — you shouldn't object either."

The voice asked sharply, "What do you mean?"

Gefty said, "Shut the control unit off. From what you were saying, that throws us automatically back into norm-space, while we're still close enough to the Hub. You'll find plenty of people there who'll stake you to a trip to the future if they can go along and are convinced they'll return. Miss Ruse and I don't happen to be that adventurous."

There was silence from the passage. Gefty added, "Take your time to make up your mind about it, if you want to. I don't like the idea of those lights hitting us, but neither do you. And I think I can wait this out as well as you can. . . ."

The silence stretched out. Presently Gefty said, "If you do accept, slide that fire-shooting device of yours into the room before you show up. We don't want accidents."

He paused again. Kerim was chewing her lips, hands clenched into small fists in her lap. Then Maulbow answered, voice flat and expressionless now.

"The worst thing we can do at present," he said, "is to prolong a dispute about possible courses of action. If I disarm, will you lay aside your gun?"

"Yes."

"Then I accept your conditions, disappointing as they are."

He was silent. After a moment, Gefty heard the white rod clatter lightly along the floor of the passage. It struck the passage wall, spun off it, and rolled into the instrument room, coming to rest a few feet away from him. Gefty hesitated, picked it up and laid it on the wall table. He placed his own gun beside it, moved a dozen steps away. Kerim's eyes followed him anxiously.

"Gefty," she whispered, "he might . . ."

Gefty looked at her, formed the words "It's all right" with his mouth and called, "Guns have been put aside, Maulbow. Come on in, and let's keep it peaceable."

He waited, arms hanging loosely at his side, heart beating heavily, as quick footsteps came up the passage. Maulbow appeared in the entrance, glanced at Gefty and Kerim, then about the room. His gaze rested for a moment on the wall table, shifted back to Gefty. Maulbow came on into the room, turning towards Gefty, mouth twisting.

He said softly, "It is not our practice, Rammer, to share the secrets of the Great Current with other races. I hadn't foreseen that you might become a dangerous nuisance. But now —"

His right hand began to lift, half closed about some small golden instrument. Gefty's left arm moved back and quickly forwards.

The service knife slid out of its sheath and up from his palm as an arrow of smoky blackness burst from the thing in Maulbow's hand. The blackness came racing with a thin, snarling noise across the floor towards Gefty's feet. The knife flashed above it, turning, and stood hilt-deep in Maulbow's chest.

Gefty returned a few minutes later from the forward cabin which served as the *Queen's* sick bay, and said to Kerim, "He's still alive, though I don't know why. He may even recover. He's full of anesthetic, and that should keep him quiet till we're back in normspace. Then I'll see what we can do for him."

Kerim had lost some of her white, shocked look while he was gone. "You knew he would try to kill you?" she asked shakily.

"Suspected he had it in mind — he gave in too quick. But I thought I'd have a chance to take any gadget he was hiding away from him first. I was wrong about that. Now we'd better move fast . . ."

He switched the emergency check panel back on, glanced over the familiar patterns of lights and numbers. A few minor damage spots were indicated, but the ship was still fully operational. One minor damage spot which did not appear on the panel was now to be found in the instrument room itself, in the corner on which the door of the map room opened. The door, the adjoining bulkheads and section of flooring were scarred, blackened, and as assortedly malodorous as burned things tend to become. That was where Gefty had stood when Maulbow entered the room, and if he had remained there an instant after letting go of the knife, he would have been in very much worse condition than the essentially fireproof furnishings.

Both Maulbow's weapons — the white rod lying innocently on the wall table and the round, golden device which had dropped from his hand spitting darts of smoking blackness — had blasted unnervingly away into that area for almost thirty seconds after Maulbow was down and twisting about on the floor. Then he went limp and the firing instantly stopped. Apparently, Maulbow's control of them had ended as he lost consciousness.

It seemed fortunate that the sick bay cabin's emergency treatment accessories, gentle as their action was, might have been designed for the specific purpose of keeping the most violent of prisoners immobilized — let alone one with a terrible knife wound in him. At the angle along which the knife had driven in and up below the ribs, an ordinary man would have been dead in seconds. But it was very evident now that Maulbow was no ordinary man, and even after the eerie weapons had been pitched out of the ship through the instrument room's disposal tube, Gefty couldn't rid himself of an uncomfortable suspicion that he wasn't done with Maulbow yet — wouldn't be done with him, in fact, until one or the other of them was dead.

He said to Kerim, "I thought the machine Maulbow set up in the storage vault would turn out to be some drive engine, but apparently it has an entirely different function. He connected it with the instruments he had made in the Hub, and together they form what he calls a control unit. The emergency panel would show if the unit were drawing juice from the ship. It isn't, and I don't know what powers it. But we do know now that the control unit is holding us in the time current, and it will go on holding us there as long as it's in operation.

"If we could shut it off, the *Queen* would be 'rejected' by the current, like Maulbow's sailer was. In other words, we'd get knocked back into normspace — which is what we want. And we want it to happen as soon as possible because, if Maulbow was telling the truth on that point, every minute that passes here is taking us farther away from the Hub, and farther from our own time towards his."

Kerim nodded, eyes intent on his face.

"Now I can't just go down there and start slapping switches around on the thing," Gefty went on. "He said it wasn't working right, and even if it were, I couldn't tell what would happen. But it doesn't seem to connect up with any ship systems — it just seems to be holding us in a field of its own. So I should be able to move the whole unit into the cargo lock and eject it from there. If we shift the *Queen* outside its field, that should have the same effect as shutting the control unit off. It should throw us back into normspace."

Kerim nodded again. "What about Mr. Maulbow's jan-andra animal?"

Gefty shrugged. "Depends on the mood I find it in. He said it wasn't usually aggressive. Maybe it isn't. I'll get into a spacesuit for protection and break out some of the mining equipment to move it along with. If I can maneuver it into an empty compartment where it will be out of the . . ."

He broke off, expression changing, eyes fastened on the emergency panel. Then he turned hurriedly, reached across the side of the console for the intership airseal controls. Kerim asked apprehensively, "What's the matter, Gefty?"

"Wish I knew . . . exactly." Gefty indicated the emergency panel. "Little red light there, on the storage deck section — it wasn't showing a minute ago. It means that the vault doors have been opened since then."

He saw the same half-superstitious fear appear in her face that had touched him. "You think *he* did it?"

"I don't know." Maulbow's control of the guns had seemed uncanny enough. But that was a different matter. The guns were a product of his own time and science. But the vault door mechanisms? There might have been sufficient opportunity for Maulbow to study them and alter them, for some purpose of his own, since he'd come aboard. . . .

"I've got the ship compartments and decks sealed off from each other now," Gefty said slowly. "The only connecting points from one to the other are personnel hatches — they're small air locks. So the janandra's confined to the storage deck. If it's come out of the vault, it might be a nuisance until I can get equipment to handle it. But that isn't too serious. The spacesuits are on the second deck, and I'll get into one before I go on to the storage. You wait here a moment, I'll look in on Maulbow again before I start."

If Maulbow wasn't still unconscious, he was doing a good job of feigning it. Gefty looked at the pale, lax face, the half-shut eyes, shook his head and left the cabin, locking it behind him. It mightn't be Maulbow's doing, but having the big snake loose in the storage could, in fact, make things extremely awkward now. He didn't think his gun would make much impression on anything of that size, and while several of the ship's mining tools could be employed as very effective close-range weapons, they happened, unfortunately, to be stored away on the same deck.

He found Kerim standing in the center of the instrument room, waiting for him.

"Gefty," she said, "do you notice anything? An odd sort of smell. . . ."

Then the odor was in Gefty's nostrils, too, and the back of his neck turned to ice as he recognized it. He glanced up at the ventilation outlet, looked back at Kerim.

He took her arm, said softly, "Come this way. Keep very quiet! I don't know how it happened, but the janandra's on the main deck now. That's what it smells like. The smell's coming through the ventilation system, so the thing's moving around in the port section. We'll go the other way."

Kerim whispered, "What will we do?"

"Get ourselves into spacesuits first, and then get Maulbow's control unit out of the ship. The janandra may be looking around for him. If it is, it won't bother us."

He hadn't wanted to remind Kerim that, from what Maulbow said, there might be more than one reason for getting rid of the control unit as quickly as possible. But it had been constantly in the back of his mind; and twice, in the few minutes that passed after Maulbow's strange weapons were silenced, he had seen a momentary pale glare apear in the unquiet flow of darkness reflecting in the viewscreens. Gefty had said nothing, because if it was true that hostile forces were alert and searching for them here, it added to their immediate danger but not at all to the absolute need to free themselves from the inexorable rush of the Great Current before they were carried beyond hope of return to their civilization.

But those brief glimpses did add to the sense of urgency throbbing in Gefty's nerves, while events, and the equally hard necessity to avoid a fatally mistaken move in this welter of unknown factors, kept blocking him. Now the mysterious manner in which Maulbow's unpleasant traveling companion had appeared on the main deck made it impossible to do anything but keep Kerim at his side. If Maulbow was still capable of taking a hand in matters, there was no reasonably safe place to leave her aboard the *Queen*.

And Maulbow might be capable of it. Twice as they hurried up the narrow, angled passages along the *Queen's* curving hull towards an airseal leading to the next compartment, Gefty caught a trace of the ammonia-like animal odor coming over the ventilating system. They reached the lock without incident; but then, as they came along the second deck hall to the ship's magazine, there was a sharp click in the stillness behind them. Its meaning was disconcertingly apparent. Gefty hesitated, turned Kerim into a side passage, guided her along it.

She looked up at his face. "It's following us?"

"Seems to be." No time for the spacesuits in the magazine now — something had just emerged from the air lock through which they had entered the second deck not many moments before. He helped the girl quickly down a section of ladderlike stairs to the airseal connecting the second deck with the storage, punched a wall button there. As the lock door opened, there was another noise from the passage they had just left, as if something had thudded briefly and heavily against one of the bulkheads. Kerim uttered a little gasp. Then they were in the lock, and Gefty slapped down two other buttons, stood watching the door behind them snap shut and, a few seconds later, the one on the far side open on the dark storage deck.

They scrambled down another twelve feet of ladder to the floor of a side passage, hearing the lock snap shut behind them. As it closed, they were in complete darkness.

Gefty seized Kerim's arm, ran with her up the passage to the left, guiding himself with his fingertips on the left bulkhead. When they came to a corner, he turned her to the left again. A few seconds later, he pulled open a small door, bundled the girl through, came in himself, and shut the door to a narrow slit behind them.

Kerim whispered shakily, "What will we do now, Gefty?"

"Stay here for the moment. It'll look for us in the vault first."

And it should go to the storage vault first where it had been guarding Maulbow's machine, to hunt for them there. But it might not. Gefty eased the gun from his pocket on the far side of Kerim. Across the dark compartment was another door. They could retreat a little farther here if it became necessary — but not very much farther.

They waited in a silence that was complete except for their unsteady breathing and the distant, deep pulse of the *Queen's* throttled-down drives. He felt Kerim trembling against him. How did Maulbow's creature move through the airseal locks? The operating mechanisms were simple — a dog might have been taught to use them. But a dog had paws. . . .

There came the soft hiss of the opening lock, the faintest shimmer of light to the right of the passage mouth he was watching through the door. A heavy thump on the floor below the locks followed, then a hard click as the lock closed and complete darkness returned.

The silence resumed. Seconds dragged on. Gefty's imagination pictured the thing waiting, its great, wedge-shaped head raised as its senses probed the dark about it for a sign of the two human beings. Then a vague rushing noise began, growing louder as it approached the passage mouth, crossing it, receding rapidly again to the left.

Gefty let his breath out slowly, eased the door open and stood listening again. Abruptly, there was reflected light in the lock passage, coming now from the left. He said in a whisper, "It's moving around in the main hall, Kerim. We can go on the other way now, but we'll have to be fast and keep quiet. I've thought of how we can get rid of that thing."

The cargo lock on the storage deck had two inner doors. The one which opened into the side of the vault hall was built to allow passage of the largest chunks of freight the *Queen* was likely to be burdened with; it was almost thirty feet wide and twenty high. The second door was just large enough to let a man in a spacesuit climb in and out of the side of the lock without using the freight door. It opened on a tiny control cubicle from which the lock's mechanisms were operated during loading processes.

Gefty let Kerim and himself into the cubicle from one of the passages, steered the girl through the pitch blackness of the little room to the chair before the control panel and told her to sit down. He groped for a moment at the side of the panel, found a knob and twisted it. There was a faint click. A scattering of pale lights appeared suddenly on the panel, a dark viewscreen, set at a tilt above them, reflecting their gleam.

Gefty explained in a low voice, "Left side of that screen covers the lock. Right one covers the big hall outside. No lights in either at the moment, so you don't see anything. Only way the cargo door to the hall can be opened or closed is with these switches right here. What I want to do is get the janandra into the lock, slam the door on it and lock down the control switches. Then we've got it trapped."

"But how are you going to get it to go in there?"

"No real problem — I'll be three jumps ahead of it. Then I duck back up into this cubicle, and lock both doors. And it'll be inside the lock. You have the picture now?"

Kerim said unsteadily, "I do. But it sounds awfully risky, Gefty."

"Well, I don't like it either," Gefty admitted. "So I'll start right now before I lose my nerve. As soon as I move out into the vault hall, the lighting will go on. That's automatic. You watch the right side of the screen. If you see the janandra coming before I do, yell as loud as you can."

He shifted the two inner door switches to the right. A red spark appeared in the dark viewscreen, high up near the center. A second red light showed on the cubicle bulkhead beside Gefty. Beneath it an oblong section of the bulkhead turned silently away on heavy hinges, became a door two feet in thickness, which stood jutting out at a right angle into the darkness of the cargo lock. A wave of cold air moved through it into the control cubicle.

On the screen, another red spark appeared beside the first one.

"Both doors are open now," Gefty murmured to the girl. "The janandra isn't in the vault hall or the lighting would have turned on, but it may have heard the door open and be on its way. So keep watching the screen."

"I certainly will!" she whispered shakily.

Gefty took an oversized wrench from the wall, climbed quickly and quietly down the three ladder steps to the floor of the lock, and walked across it to the sill of the giant freight door, which now had swung out and down into the vault hall, fitting itself into a depression of the flooring. He hesitated an instant on the sill, then stepped out into the big dark hall. Light filled it immediately in both directions.

He stood quiet, intent on the storage vault entrance far

up the hall to his left. He could see the vault was open. The janandra might still be inside it. But the seconds passed, and the dark entrance remained silent and there was no suggestion of motion beyond it. Gefty glanced to the right, moved a dozen steps farther out into the hall, hefted the wrench and spun it through the air towards the ventilator frame on the opposite bulkhead.

The heavy tool clanged loudly against the frame, bounced off and thudded to the floor. Gefty started slowly over to it, heart pounding, with the vault entrance still at the edge of his vision.

Kerim's voice screamed, "*Gefty, it's —*"

He spun around, sprinted back to the cargo lock. The janandra had come silently out of the nearest side passage behind him, was approaching with the remembered oiling swiftness of motion, its great head lifted a yard from the floor. Gefty plunged through the lock, jumped for the top of the cubicle door steps, came stumbling into the cubicle. Kerim was on her feet, staring. He swung the cubicle door switch to the left, slapping it flat to the panel. The door snapped back into the wall behind him with a force that shook the floor.

On the screen, the janandra's thick, dark worm-shape was swinging around in the dim lock to regain the open hall. It had seen the trap. But the freight door switch went flat beside the other, and the freight door rose with massive swiftness. The heavy body smashed against it, went sliding back to the floor as the door slammed shut and the screen section showing the cargo lock turned dark.

"Got it — got it — got it!" Gefty heard himself whispering exultantly. He switched on the lock's interior lights.

Then he swore softly, and, beside him, Kerim sucked in her breath.

*   *   *

The screen showed the janandra in violent but apparently purposeful motion inside the lock . . . and it was also apparent now that it was a more complexly constructed creature than the long worm-body and heavy head had indicated. The skin, to a distance of some eight feet back of the head, had spread out into a wide, flexible frill. From beneath the frill extended half a dozen jointed, bone-white arms, along with waving, ribbonlike appendages less easy to define. The thing was reared half up along the hall door, inspecting its surface with these members; then suddenly it flung itself around and flashed over to the outer lock door. Three arms shot out; wiry fingers caught the three spin-locks simultaneously, began to whirl them.

Gefty said, staring, "Kerim, it's going to . . ."

The janandra didn't. The motion checked suddenly, was reversed. The locks drew tight again. The janandra swung back from the door, lifting half its length upwards, big head weaving about as it inspected the tool racks overhead. An arm reached suddenly, snatched something from one of the racks. Then the thing turned again; and in the next instant its head filled the viewscreen. Kerim made a choked sound of fright, jerking back against Gefty. The bulging, metal-green eyes seemed to stare directly at him. And the screen went black.

Kerim whispered, "Wha . . . what happened, Gefty?"

Gefty swallowed, said, "It smashed the view pickup. Must have guessed we were watching and didn't like it. . . ." He added, "I was beginning to think Maulbow must be some kind of superman. But it wasn't any remote-control magic of his that let the janandra out of the vault, and opened the intership locks when it came up to the main deck and followed us down again. It was doing all that for itself. It's Maulbow's partner, not his pet. And it's probably got at least as good a brain as anyone else on board behind that ugly face."

Kerim moistened her lips. "Can it . . . could it get out again?"

"Into the ship?" Gefty shook his head decidedly. "Uh-uh. It could dump itself out on the other side — and it almost did before it realized where it was and what it was about to do. But the inner lock doors won't open until someone opens them right on this panel. No, the thing's safely trapped. On the other hand . . ."

On the other hand, Gefty realized that he wouldn't now be able to bring himself to eject the janandra out of the cargo lock and into the Great Current. Its intentions obviously hadn't been friendly, but its level of intelligence was as good as his own, and perhaps somewhat better; and at present it was helpless. To dispose of it as he'd had in mind would therefore be the cold-blooded murder of an equal. But so long as that ugly and formidable shipmate of Maulbow's stayed in the cargo lock, the lock couldn't be used to get rid of the control unit in the vault.

A new solution presented itself while Gefty was making a rapid and rather desperate mental review of various heavy-duty tools which might be employed as weapons to force the janandra into submission and haul it off for confinement elsewhere in the ship. Not impossible, but a highly precarious and time-consuming operation at best. Then another thought occurred: the storage vault lay directly against the hull of the *Queen* —

How long to cut through the hull? The ship's mining equipment was on board, and the tools were self-powered. Climb into a spacesuit, empty the air from the entire storage deck, leaving the janandra imprisoned in the cargo lock . . . with Maulbow incapacitated in sick bay, and Kerim back in the control compartment and also in a suit, for additional protection. Then cut ship's power to this deck to avoid complications with the *Queen's* involved circuitry and work under space conditions — half an hour if he hurried.

"**S**houldn't take more than another ten minutes," he informed Kerim presently over the suit's intercom.

"I'm very glad to hear it, Gefty." She sounded shaky.

"Anything going on in the screens?" he asked.

She hesitated a little, said, "No. Not at the moment."

Gefty grunted, blinked sweat from his eyes, and took hold of the handgrips of the heavy mining cutter again, turning it nose down towards the vault floor. The guide light found the point he was working on, and the slice beam stabbed out, began nibbling delicately away to extend the curving line it had eaten through the *Queen's* thick skin. He had drawn a twenty-five foot circle around Maulbow's battered control unit and the instruments attached to it, well outside the fragile-looking safety field. The circle was broken at four points where he would plant explosives. The explosives, going off together, should shatter the connecting links with the hull and throw the machine clear. If that didn't release them immediately from its influence, he would see what putting the *Queen's* drives into action would do.

"Gefty?" Kerim's voice asked.

"Uh-huh?"

He could hear her swallow over the intercom. "Those lights are back now."

"How many?"

"Two," Kerim said. "I *think* they're only two. They keep crossing back and forth in front of us." She laughed nervously. "It's idiotic, of course, but I do get the feeling they're looking at us."

Gefty said hesitantly, "Everything's set but I need another minute or two to get this last connection whittled down a little more. If I blow the charge too soon, it mightn't take the gadget clean out of the ship."

Kerim said, "I know. I'll just watch . . . they just disappeared again." Her voice changed. "Now there's something else."

"What's that?"

"You know you said to watch the cargo lock lights on the emergency panel."

"Yes."

"The outer lock door has just been opened."

"What!"

"It must have been. The light started blinking red just now as I was looking at it."

Gefty was silent a moment, his mind racing. Why would the janandra open the lock? From what Maulbow had said, it could live for a while without air, but it still could gain nothing but eventual death from leaving the ship —

Unless, Gefty thought, the janandra had become aware in some way that he was about to blow their machine out of the *Queen*. There were grappling lines in the cargo lock, and if four or five of those lines were slapped to the circular section of the hull he'd loosened . . .

"Kerim," he said.

"Yes?"

"I'm going to blow the deal right now. Got your suit snapped to the wall braces like I showed you?"

"Yes, Gefty." Her voice was faint but clear.

He turned the cutter away from the line it had dug, sent it rolling off towards the far wall. He hurried around the circle, checking the four charges, lumbered over to the vault passage, stopped just around the corner. He took the firing box from his suit.

"Ready, Kerim?" He opened the box.

"Ready. . . ."

"Here goes!" Gefty reached into the box, twisted the firing handle. Light flared in the vault. The deck shook below him. He came stumbling out from behind the wall.

Maulbow's machine and its stand of instruments had vanished. Where it had stood was a dark circular hole. Nothing else seemed to have happened. Gefty clumped hurriedly over to the mining cutter, swung it around, started more cautiously back towards the hole. He didn't have the faintest idea what would come next, but a definite possibility was that he would see the janandra's dark form flowing up over the rim of the hole. Letting it run into the cutter beam might be the best way to discourage it from re-entering the *Queen*.

Instead, a dazzling brilliance suddenly blotted out everything. The cutter was plucked from Gefty's grasp; then he was picked up, suit and all, and slammed up towards the vault ceiling. He had a feeling that inaudible thunders were shaking the ship. He seemed to be rolling over and over along the ceiling. At last, the suit crashed into something which showed a total disinclination to yield, and Gefty blacked out.

The left side of his face felt pushed out of shape; his left eye wasn't functioning too well, and there was a severe pulsing ache throughout the top of his head. But Gefty felt happy.

There were a few qualifying considerations.

"Of course," he pointed out to Kerim, "all we can really say immediately is that we're back in normspace and somewhere in the galaxy."

She smiled shakily. "Isn't that saying quite a lot, Gefty?"

"It's something." Gefty glanced around the instrument room. He had placed an emergency light on the console, but except for that, the control compartment was in darkness. The renewed battering the *Queen* had absorbed had knocked out the power in the forward section. The viewscreens were black, every instrument dead. But he'd seen the stars of normspace through the torn vault floor. It was something. . . .

"We might have the light that slugged us to thank for that," he said. "I'm not sure just what did happen there, but it could have been Maulbow's control unit it was attacking rather than the ship. Maulbow said the lights were sensitive to the unit. At any rate, we're here, and we're rid of the gadget — and of the janandra." He hesitated. "I just don't feel you should get your hopes too high. We may find out we're a very long way from the Hub."

Kerim's large eyes showed a degree of confidence which made him almost uncomfortable. "If we are," she said serenely, "you'll get us back somehow."

Gefty cleared his throat. "Well, we'll see. If the power shutoff is something the *Queen's* repair scanners can handle, the instruments will come back on any minute. Give the scanners ten minutes. If they haven't done it by that time, they can't do it and I'll have to play repairman. Then, with the instruments working, we can determine exactly where we are."

Unless, he told himself silently, they'd wound up in a distant cluster never penetrated by the Federation's mapping teams. And there was the other little question of where they now were in time. But Kerim looked rosy with relief, and those details could wait.

He took up another emergency light, switched it on and said, "I'll see how Maulbow is doing while we're waiting for power. If the first aid treatment has pulled him through so far, the autosurgeon probably can fix him up."

Kerim's face suddenly took on a guilty expression. "I forgot all about Mr. Maulbow!" She hesitated. "Should I come along?"

Gefty shook his head. "I won't need help. And if it's a case for the surgeon, you wouldn't like it. Those things work painlessly, but it gets to be a mess for a while."

He shut off the light again when he reached the sick bay which was running on its independent power system. As he opened the cabin door from the dispensary, carrying the autosurgeon, it became evident that Maulbow was still alive but that he might be in delirium. Gefty placed the surgeon on the table, went over to the bed and looked at Maulbow.

To the extent that the emergency treatment instruments' cautious restraints permitted, Maulbow was twisting slowly about on the bed. He was speaking in a low, rapid voice, his face distorted by emotion. The words were not slurred, but they were in a language Gefty didn't know. It seemed clear that Maulbow had reverted mentally to his own time, and for some seconds he remained unaware that Gefty had entered the room. Then, surprisingly, the slitted blue eyes opened wider and focused on Gefty's face. And Maulbow screamed with rage.

Gefty felt somewhat disconcerted. For the reason alone that he was under anesthetic, Maulbow should not have been conscious. But he was. The words were now ones Gefty could understand, and Maulbow was telling him things which would have been interesting enough under different circumstances. Gefty broke in as soon as he could.

"Look," he said quietly, "I'm trying to help you. I . . ."

Maulbow interrupted him in turn, not at all quietly. Gefty listened a moment longer, then shrugged. So Maulbow didn't like him. He couldn't say honestly that he'd ever liked Maulbow much, and what he was hearing made him like Maulbow considerably less. But he would keep the man from the future alive if he could.

He positioned the autosurgeon behind the head of the bed to allow the device to begin its analysis, stood back at its controls where he could both follow the progress it made and watch Maulbow without exciting him further by remaining within his range of vision. After a moment, the surgeon shut off the first-aid instruments and made unobtrusive use of a heavy tranquilizing drug. Then it waited.

Maulbow should have lapsed into passive somnolence thirty seconds afterwards. But the drug seemed to produce no more effect on him mentally than the preceding anesthetic. He raged and screeched on. Gefty watched him uneasily, knowing now that he was looking at insanity. There was nothing more he could do at the moment — the autosurgeon's decisions were safer than any nonprofessional's guesswork. And the surgeon continued to wait.

Then, abruptly, Maulbow died. The taut body slumped against the bed and the contorted features relaxed. The eyes remained half open; and when Gefty came around to the side of the bed, they still seemed to be looking up at him, but they no longer moved. A thin trickle of blood started from the side of the slack mouth and stopped again.

*　　　*　　　*

The control compartment was still darkened and without power when Gefty returned to it. He told Kerim briefly what had happened, added, "I'm not at all sure now he was even human. I'd rather believe he wasn't."

"Why that, Gefty?" She was studying his expression soberly.

Gefty hesitated, said, "I thought at first he was furious because we'd upset his plans. But they weren't his plans . . . they were the janandra's. He wasn't exactly its servant. I suppose you'd have to say he was something like a pet animal."

Kerim said incredulously, "But that isn't possible! Think of how intelligently Mr. Maulbow . . ."

"He was following instructions," Gefty said. "The janandra let him know whatever it wanted done. He was following instructions again when he tried to kill me after I'd got away from the thing in the vault. The real brain around here was the janandra . . . and it was a real brain. With a little luck it would have had the ship."

Kerim smiled briefly. "You handled that big brain rather well, I think."

"I was the one who got lucky," Gefty said. "Anyway, where Maulbow came from, it's the janandra's kind that gives the orders. And the thing is, Maulbow liked it that way. He didn't want it to be different. When the light hit us, it killed the janandra on the outside of the ship. Maulbow felt it happen and it cracked him up. He wanted to kill us for it. But since he was helpless, he killed himself. He didn't want to be healed — not by us. At least, that's what it looks like."

He shrugged, checked his watch, climbed out of the chair. "Well," he said, "the ten minutes I gave the *Queen* to turn the power back on are up. Looks like the old girl couldn't do it. So I'll —"

The indirect lighting system in the instrument room went on silently. The emergency light flickered and went out. Gefty's head came around.

Kerim was staring past him at the screens, her face radiant.

"Oh, Gefty!" she cried softly. "Oh, Gefty! Our stars!"

"Green dot here is us," Gefty explained, somewhat hoarsely. He cleared his throat, went on, "Our true ship position, that is — " He stopped, realizing he was talking too much, almost babbling, in an attempt to take some of the tension out of the moment. The next few seconds might not tell them where they were, but it would show whether they had been carried beyond the regions of space charted by Federation instruments. Which would mean the difference between having a chance — whether a good chance or a bad one — of getting home eventually, and the alternative of being hopelessly lost.

There had been nothing recognizably familiar about the brilliantly dense star patterns in the viewscreens, but he gave no further thought to that. Unless the ship's exact position was known or one was on an established route, it was a waste of time looking for landmarks in a sizable cluster.

He turned on the basic star chart. Within the locator plate the green pinpoint of light reappeared, red-ringed and suspended now against the three-dimensional immensities of the Milky Way. It stayed still a moment, began a smooth drift towards Galactic East. Gefty let his breath out carefully. He sensed Kerim's eyes on him but kept his gaze fixed on the locator plate.

The green dot slowed, came to a stop. Gefty's finger tapped the same button four times. The big chart flicked out of existence, and in the plate three regional star maps appeared and vanished in quick succession behind it. The fourth map stayed. For a few seconds, the red-circled green spark was not visible here. Then it showed at the eastern margin of the map, came gliding forwards and to the left, slowed again and held steady. Now the star map began to glide through the locator plate, carrying the fixed green dot with it. It brought the dot up to dead center point in the locator plate and stopped.

Gefty slumped a little. He rubbed his hands slowly down his face and muttered a few words. Then he shook his head.

"Gefty," Kerim whispered, "what is it? Where are we?"

Gefty looked at her.

"After we got hauled into that time current," he said hoarsely, "I tried to find out which way in space we were headed. The direction indicators over there seemed to show we were trying to go everywhere at once. You remember Maulbow's control unit wasn't working right, needed adjustments. Well, all those little impulses must have pretty well canceled out because we weren't taken really far. In the last hour and a half we've covered roughly the distance the *Queen* could have gone on her own in, say, thirty days."

"Then where . . ."

"Home," Gefty said simply. "It's ridiculous! Other side of the Hub from where we started." He nodded at the plate. "Eastern Hub Quadrant. Section Six Eight. The G2 behind the green dot — that's the Evalee system. We could be putting down at Evalee Interstellar three hours from now if we wanted to."

Kerim was laughing and crying together. "Oh, Gefty! I knew you would . . ."

"A fat lot I had to do with it!" Gefty leaned forward suddenly, switched on the transmitter. "And now let's pick up a live newscast. There's something else I . . ."

His voice trailed off. The transmitter screen lit up with a blurred jumble of print, colors, a muttering of voices, music and noises. Gefty twisted a dial. The screen cleared, showed a newscast headline sheet. Gefty blinked at it, glanced sideways at Kerim, grimaced.

"The something else," he said, his voice a little strained, "was something I was also worried about. Looks like I was more or less right."

"Why, what's wrong?"

"Nothing really bad," Gefty assured her. He added, "I think. But take a look at the Federation dateline."

Kerim peered at the screen, frowned. "But . . ."

"Uh-huh."

"Why, that . . . that's almost . . ."

"That," Gefty said, "or rather *this* is the day after we started out from the Hub, headed roughly Galactic west. Three weeks ago. We'd be just past Miam." He knuckled his chin. "Interesting thought, isn't it?"

Kerim was silent for long seconds. "Then they . . . or we . . ."

"Oh, they're us, all right," Gefty said. "They'd have to be, wouldn't they?"

"I suppose so. It seems a little confusing. But I was thinking. If you send them a transmitter call . . ."

Gefty shook his head. "The *Queen's* transmitter isn't too hot, but it might push a call as far as Evalee. Then we could arrange for a Com-Web link-up there, and in another ten minutes or so . . . but I don't think we'd better."

"Why not?" Kerim demanded.

"Because we got through it all safely, so we're going to get through it safely. But if we receive that message now and never go on to Maulbow's moon . . . you see? There's no way of knowing just what would happen."

Kerim looked hesitant, frowned. "I suppose you're right," she agreed reluctantly at last. "So Mr. Maulbow will have to stay dead now. And that janandra." After a moment she added pensively, "Of course, they weren't really very nice —"

Gefty shivered. One of the things he'd learned from Maulbow's ravings was the real reason he and Kerim had been taken along on the trip. He didn't feel like telling Kerim about it just yet, but it had been solely because of Maulbow's concern for his master's creature comforts. The janandra could go for a long time without food, but after fasting for several years on the moon, a couple of snacks on the homeward run would have been highly welcome.

And the janandra was a gourmet. It much preferred, as Maulbow well knew, to have its snacks still wriggling-fresh as it started them down its gullet.

"No," Gefty said, "I couldn't call either of them really nice."

LION LOOSE

1

For twelve years, at a point where three major shipping routes of the Federation of the Hub crossed within a few hours' flight of one another, the Seventh Star Hotel had floated in space, a great golden sphere, gleaming softly in the void through its translucent shells of battle plastic. The Star had been designed to be much more than a convenient transfer station for travelers and freight; for some years after it was opened to the public, it retained a high rating among the more exotic pleasure resorts of the Hub. The Seventh Star Hotel was the place to have been that season, and the celebrities and fat cats converged on it with their pals and hangers-on. The Star blazed with life, excitement, interstellar scandals, tinkled with streams of credits dancing in from a thousand worlds. In short, it had started out as a paying proposition.

But gradually things changed. The Star's entertainment remained as delightfully outrageous as ever; the cuisine as excellent; the accommodations and service were still above reproach. The fleecing, in general, became no less expertly painless. But one had *been* there. By its eighth year, the Star was dated. Now, in its twelfth, it lived soberly off the liner and freighter trade, four fifths of the guest suites shut down, the remainder irregularly occupied between ship departures.

And in another seven hours, if the plans of certain men went through, the Seventh Star Hotel would abruptly wink out of existence.

*　　　*　　　*

Some fifty or sixty early diners were scattered about the tables on the garden terraces of Phalagon House, the Seventh Star Hotel's most exclusive eatery. One of them had just finished his meal, sat smoking and regarding a spiraling flow of exquisitely indicated female figures across the garden's skyscape with an air of friendly approval. He was a large and muscular young man, deeply tanned, with shoulders of impressive thickness, an aquiline nose, and dark, reflective eyes.

After a minute or two, he yawned comfortably, put out the cigarette, and pushed his chair back from the table. As he came to his feet, there was a soft bell-note from the table ComWeb. He hesitated, said, "Go ahead."

"Is intrusion permitted?" the ComWeb inquired.

"Depends," the guest said. "Who's calling?"

"The name is Reetal Destone."

He grinned, appeared pleasantly surprised. "Put the lady through."

There was a brief silence. Then a woman's voice inquired softly, "Quillan?"

"Right here, doll! Where —"

"Seal the ComWeb, Quillan."

He reached down to the instrument, tapped the seal button, said, "All right. We're private."

"Probably," the woman's voice said. "But better scramble this, too. I want to be very sure no one's listening"

Quillan grunted, slid his left hand into an inner coat pocket, briefly fingered a device of the approximate size and shape of a cigarette, drew his hand out again. "Scrambling!" he announced. "Now, what —"

"Mayday, Quillan," the soft voice said. "Can you come

immediately?"

Quillan's face went expressionless. "Of course. Is it urgent?"

"I'm in no present danger. But we'd better waste no time."

"Is it going to take real hardware? I'm carrying a finger gun at the moment."

"Then go to your rooms and pick up something useful," Reetal said. "This should take real hardware, all right."

"All right. Then where do I go?"

"I'll meet you at your door. I know where it is."

When Quillan arrived, she was standing before the door to his suite, a tall blonde in a sleeveless black and gold sheath; a beautiful body, a warm, lovely, humorous face. The warmth and humor were real, but masked a mind as impersonally efficient as a computer, and a taste for high and dangerous living. When Quillan had last met Reetal Destone, a year and a half before, the taste was being satisfied in industrial espionage. He hadn't heard of her activities since then.

She smiled thoughtfully at him as he came up. "I'll wait outside," she said. "We're not talking here."

Quillan nodded, went on into his living room, selected a gun belt and holstered gun from a suitcase, fastened the belt around his waist under the coat, and came out. "Now what?"

"First a little portal-hopping —"

He followed her across the corridor and into a tube portal, watched as she tapped out a setting. The exit light flashed a moment later; they stepped out into a vacant lounge elsewhere in the same building, crossed it, entered another portal. After three more shifts, they emerged into a long hall, dimly lit, heavily carpeted. There was no one in sight.

"Last stop," Reetal said. She glanced up at his face. "We're on the other side of the Star now, in one of the sections they've closed up. I've established a kind of emergency headquarters here. The Star's nearly broke, did you know?"

"I'd heard of it."

"That appears to be part of the reason for what's going on."

Quillan said, "What's going on?"

Reetal slid her arm through his, said, "Come on. That's my, hm-m-m, unregistered suite over there. Big boy, it's very, very selfish of me, but I was extremely glad to detect your name on the list of newly arrived guests just now! As to what's going on . . . the *Camelot* berths here at midnight, you know."

Quillan nodded. "I've some business with one of her passengers."

Reetal bent to unlock the entrance door to the indicated suite. "The way it looks now," she remarked, "the odds are pretty high that you're not going to keep that appointment."

"Why not?"

"Because shortly after the *Camelot* docks and something's been unloaded from her, the *Camelot* and the Seventh Star Hotel are scheduled to go *poof!* together. Along with you, me, and some twelve thousand other people. And, so far, I haven't been able to think of a good way to keep it from happening."

Quillan was silent a moment. "Who's scheduling the poof?" he asked.

"Some old acquaintances of ours are among them. Come on in. What they're doing comes under the heading of destroying the evidence."

*　　　*　　　*

She locked the door behind them, said, "Just a moment," went over to the paneled wall, turned down a tiny silver switch. "Room portal," she said, nodding at the wall. "It might come in handy. I keep it turned off most of the time."

"Why are you turning it on now?" Quillan asked.

"One of the Star's stewards is working on this with me. He'll be along as soon as he can get away. Now I'll give you the whole thing as briefly as I can. The old acquaintances I mentioned are some boys of the Brotherhood of Beldon. Movaine's here; he's got Marras Cooms and Fluel with him, and around thirty of the Brotherhood's top guns. Nome Lancion's coming in on the *Camelot* in person tonight to take charge. Obviously, with all that brass on the job, they're after something very big. Just what it is, I don't yet know. I've got one clue, but a rather puzzling one. Tell you about that later. Do you know Velladon?"

"The commodore here?" Quillan nodded. "I've never met him but I know who he is."

Reetal said, "He's been manager of the Seventh Star Hotel for the past nine years. He's involved in the Beldon outfit's operation. So is the chief of the Star's private security force — his name's Ryter — and half a dozen other Star executives. They've got plenty of firepower, too; close to half the entire security force, I understand, including all the officers. That would come to nearly seventy men. There's reason to believe the rest of the force was disarmed and murdered by them in the subspace section of the Star about twelve hours ago. They haven't been seen since then.

"Now, Velladon, aside from his share in whatever they're after, has another reason for wanting to wipe out the Star in an unexplained blowup. There I have definite information. Did you know the Mooley brothers owned the Star?"

"Yes."

"I've been working for the Mooleys the past eight months," Reetal said, "checking up on employees at Velladon's level for indications of graft. And it appears the commodore has been robbing them blind here for at least several years."

"Sort of risky thing to try with the Mooleys, from what I hear," Quillan remarked.

"Yes. Very. Velladon had reason to be getting a little desperate about that. Two men were planted here a month ago. One of them is Sher Heraga, the steward I told you about. The other man came in as a bookkeeper. Two weeks ago, Heraga got word out that the bookkeeper had disappeared. Velladon and Ryter apparently got wise to what he was trying to do. So the Mooleys sent me here to find out exactly what was going on before they took action. I arrived four days ago."

She gave a regretful little headshake. "I waited almost a day before contacting Heraga. It seemed advisable to move very cautiously in the matter. But that made it a little too late to do anything. Quillan, for the past three days, the Seventh Star Hotel has been locked up like a bank vault. And except for ourselves, only the people who are in on the plot are aware of it."

"The message transmitters are inoperative?" he asked.

Reetal nodded. "The story is that a gravitic storm center in the area has disrupted transmissions completely for the time being."

"What about incoming ships?"

"Yours was the only one scheduled before the *Camelot* arrives. It left again eight hours ago. Nobody here had been let on board. The guests who wanted to apply for outgoing berths were told there were none open, that they'd have to wait for the *Camelot*."

She went over to a desk, unlocked a drawer, took out a sheaf of papers, and handed one of them to Quillan. "That's the layout of the Star," she said. "This five-level building over by the shell is the Executive Block. The Brotherhood and the commodore's men moved in there this morning. The Block is the Star's defense center. It's raid-proofed, contains the control offices and the transmitter and armament rooms. About the standard arrangement. While they hold the Executive Block, they have absolute control of the Star."

"If it's the defense center, it should be practically impossible to do anything about them there," Quillan agreed. "They could close it up, and dump the air out of the rest of the Star in a minute, if they had to. But there must be . . . well, what about the lifeboats in the subspace section — and our pals must have a getaway ship stashed away somewhere?"

"They have two ships," Reetal said. "A souped-up armed freighter the Brotherhood came in on, and a large armed yacht which seems to be the commodore's personal property. Unfortunately, they're both in subspace locks."

"Why unfortunately?"

"Because they've sealed off subspace. Try portaling down there, and you'll find yourself looking at a battle-plastic bulkhead. There's no way of getting either to those ships or to the lifeboats."

Quillan lifted his eyebrows. "And *that* hasn't caused any comment? What about the maintenance crews, the warehouse men, the —"

"All the work crews were hauled out of subspace this morning," Reetal said. "On the quiet, the Star's employees have been told that a gang of raiders was spotted in the warehouse area, and is at present cornered there. Naturally, the matter isn't to be mentioned to the guests, to avoid arousing unnecessary concern. And that explains everything very neatly. The absence of the security men, and why subspace is sealed off. Why the Executive Block is under guard, and can't be entered — and why the technical and office personnel in there don't come out, and don't communicate out. They've been put on emergency status, officially."

"Yunk," Quillan said disgustedly after a moment. "This begins to look like a hopeless situation, doll!"

"True."

"Let's see now —"

Reetal interrupted, "There is one portal still open to subspace. That's in the Executive Block, of course, and Heraga reports it's heavily guarded."

"How does he know?"

"The Block's getting its meals from Phalagon House. He floated a diner in there a few hours ago."

"Well," Quillan said, brightening, "perhaps a deft flavoring of poison —"

Reetal shook her head. "I checked over the hospital stocks. Not a thing there that wouldn't be spotted at once. Unless we can clobber them thoroughly, we can't afford to make them suspicious with a trick like that."

"Poison would be a bit rough on the office help, too," Quillan conceded. "They wouldn't be in on the deal."

"No, they're not. They're working under guard."

"Gas . . . no, I suppose not. It would take too long to whip up something that could turn the trick." Quillan glanced at his watch. "If the *Camelot* docks at midnight, we've around six and a half hours left, doll! And I don't find myself coming up with any brilliant ideas. What have you thought of?"

Reetal hesitated "Nothing very brilliant either," she said then. "But there are two things we might try as a last resort."

"Let's hear them."

"I know a number of people registered in the Star at present who'd be carrying personal weapons. If they were told the facts, I could probably line up around twenty who'd be willing to make a try to get into the Executive Block, and take over either the control offices or the transmitter room. If we got a warning out to the *Camelot*, that would break up the plot. Of course, it wouldn't necessarily save the Star."

"No," Quillan said, "but it's worth trying if we can't think of something better. How would you get them inside?"

"We could crowd twenty men into one of those diner trucks, and Heraga could take us in."

"What kind of people are your pals?"

"A few smugglers and confidence men I've had connections with. Fairly good boys for this sort of thing. Then there's an old millionaire sportsman, with a party of six, waiting to transfer to the *Camelot* for a safari on Jontarou. Old Philmarron isn't all there, in my opinion, but he's dead game and loves any kind of a ruckus. We can count on him and his friends, if they're not too drunk at the moment. Still . . . that's not too many to set against something less than a hundred professional guns, even though some of them must be down on the two ships."

"No, not enough." Quillan looked thoughtful. "What's the other idea?"

"Let the cat out of the bag generally. Tell the guests and the employees out here what's going on, and see if somebody can think of something that might be done."

He shook his head. "What you'd set off with that would

be anywhere between a riot and a panic. The boys in the Executive Block would simply give us the breathless treatment. Apparently, they prefer to have everything looking quiet and normal when the *Camelot* gets here —"

"But they don't have to play it that way," Reetal agreed. "We might be dead for hours before the liner docks. If they keep the landing lock closed until what they want has been unloaded, nobody on the *Camelot* would realize what had happened before it was too late."

There was a moment's silence. Then Quillan said, "You mentioned you'd picked up a clue to what they're after. What was that?"

"Well, that's a curious thing," Reetal said. "On the trip out here, a young girl name of Solvey Kinmarten attached herself to me. She didn't want to talk much, but I gathered she was newly married, and that her husband was on board and was neglecting her. She's an appealing little thing, and she seemed so forlorn and upset that I adopted her for the rest of the run. After we arrived, of course, I pretty well forgot about the Kinmartens and their troubles.

"A few hours ago, Solvey suddenly came bursting into the suite where I'm registered. She was shaking all over. After I calmed her down a bit, she spilled out her story. She and her husband, Brock Kinmarten, are rest wardens. With another man named Eltak, whom Solvey describes as `some sort of crazy old coot,' they're assigned to escort two deluxe private rest cubicles to a very exclusive sanatorium on Mezmiali. But Brock told Solvey at the beginning of the trip that this was a very unusual assignment, that he didn't want her even to come near the cubicles. That wouldn't have bothered her so much, she says, but on the way here Brock became increasingly irritable and absent-minded. She knew he was worrying about the cubicles, and she began to wonder whether they weren't involved in something illegal. The pay was very high; they're both getting almost twice the regular warden fee for the job. One day, she found an opportunity to do a little investigating.

"The cubicles are registered respectively to a Lady Pendrake and a Major Pendrake. Lady Pendrake appears to be genuine; the cubicle is unusually large and constructed somewhat differently from the ones with which Solvey was familiar, but it was clear that it had an occupant. However, the life indicator on `Major Pendrake's' cubicle registered zero when she switched it on. If there was something inside it, it wasn't a living human being.

"That was all she learned at the time, because she was afraid Brock might catch her in the cubicle room. Here in the Star, the cubicles were taken to a suite reserved for Lady Pendrake. The other man, Eltak, stayed in the suite with the cubicles, while the Kinmartens were given other quarters. However, Brock was still acting oddly and spending most of his time in the Pendrake suite. So this morning, Solvey swiped his key to the suite and slipped in when she knew the two men had left it.

"She'd barely got there when she heard Brock and Eltak at the door again. She ran into the next room, and hid in a closet. Suddenly there was a commotion in the front room, and Solvey realized that men from the Star's security force had arrived and were arresting Brock and Eltak. They hauled both of them away, then floated the cubicles out on a carrier and took them off too, locking the suite behind them.

"Solvey was in a complete panic, sure that she and Brock had become involved in some serious breach of the Warden Code. She waited a few minutes, then slipped out of the Pendrake suite, and looked me up to see if I couldn't help them. I had Heraga check, and he reported that the Kinmarten suite was under observation. Evidently, they wanted to pick up the girl, too. So I tucked her away in one of the suites in this section, and gave her something to put her to sleep. She's there now."

Quillan said, "And where are the prisoners and the cubicles?"

"In the Executive Block."

"How do you know?"

Reetal smiled briefly. "The Duke of Fluel told me."

"Huh? The Brotherhood knows you're here?"

"Relax," Reetal said. "Nobody but Heraga knows I'm working for the Mooleys. I told the Duke I had a big con deal set up when the *Camelot* came in — I even suggested he might like to get in on it. He laughed, and said he had other plans. But he won't mention to anyone that I'm here."

"Why not?"

"Because," Reetal said dryly, "what the Duke is planning to get in on is an hour of tender dalliance. Before the *Camelot* arrives, necessarily. The cold-blooded little skunk!" She hesitated a moment; when she spoke again, her voice had turned harsh and nasal, wicked amusement sounding through it. "Sort of busy at the moment, sweetheart, but we might find time for a drink or two later on in the evening, eh?"

Quillan grunted. "You're as good at the voice imitations as ever. How did you find out about the cubicles?"

"I took a chance and fed him a Moment of Truth."

"With Fluel," Quillan said thoughtfully, "that *was* taking a chance!"

"Believe me, I was aware of it! I've run into card-carrying sadists before, but the Duke's the only one who scares me silly. But it did work. He dropped in for about a minute and a half, and came out without noticing a thing. Meanwhile, I'd got the answers to a few questions. The bomb with which they're planning to mop up behind them already has been planted up here in the norm-space section. Fluel didn't know where; armaments experts took care of it. It's armed now. There's a firing switch on each of their ships, and both switches have to be tripped before the thing goes off. Part of what they're after is in those Pendrake rest cubicles —"

"Part of it?" Quillan asked.

"Uh-huh. An even hundred similar cubicles will be unloaded from the *Camelot* — the bulk of the haul; which is why Nome Lancion is supervising things on the liner. I started to ask what was in the cubicles, but I saw Fluel was beginning to lose that blank look they have under Truth, and switched back to light chitchat just before he woke up. Yaco's paying for the job — or rather, it *will* pay for the stuff, on delivery, and no questions asked."

"That's not very much help, is it?" Quillan said after a moment. "Something a big crooked industrial combine like Yaco thinks it can use —"

"It must expect to be able to use it to extremely good advantage," Reetal said. "The Brotherhood will collect thirty million credits for their part of the operation. The commodore's group presumably won't do any worse." She glanced past Quillan toward the room portal. "It's O.K., Heraga! Come in."

Sher Heraga was a lean, dark-skinned little man with a badly bent nose, black curly hair, and a nervous look. He regretted, he said, that he hadn't been able to uncover anything which might be a lead to the location of the bomb. Apparently, it wasn't even being guarded. And, of course, a bomb of the size required here would be quite easy to conceal.

"If they haven't placed guards over it," Reetal agreed, "it'll take blind luck to spot it! Unless we can get hold of one of the men who knows where it's planted —"

There was silence for some seconds. Then Quillan said, "Well, if we can't work out a good plan, we'd better see what we can do with one of the bad ones. Are the commodore's security men wearing uniforms?"

Heraga shook his head. "Not the ones I saw."

"Then here's an idea," Quillan said. "As things stand, barging into the Executive Block with a small armed group can't accomplish much. It might be more interesting than sitting around and waiting to be blown up, but it still would be suicide. However, if we could get things softened up and disorganized in there first —"

"Softened up and disorganized how?" Reetal asked.

"We can use that notion you had of having Heraga float in another diner. This time, I'm on board — in a steward's uniform, in case the guards check."

"They didn't the first time," Heraga said.

"Sloppy of them. Well, they're just gun hands. Anyway, once we're inside I shuck off the uniform and get out. Heraga delivers his goodies, and leaves again —"

Reetal gave him a look. "You'll get shot down the instant you're seen, dope!"

"I think not. There're two groups in there — around a hundred men in all — and they haven't had time to get well acquainted yet. I'll have my gun in sight, and anyone who sees me should figure I belong to the other group, until I run into one of the Brotherhood boys who knows me personally."

"Then that's when you get shot down. I understand the last time you and the Duke of Fluel met, he woke up with lumps."

"The Duke doesn't love me," Quillan admitted. "But there's nothing personal between me and Movaine or Marras Cooms — and I'll have a message for Movaine."

"What kind of a message?"

"I'll have to play that by ear a little. It depends on how things look in there. But I have a few ideas, based on what you've learned of the operation. Now, just what I can do when I get that far, I don't know yet. I'll simply try to louse the deal up as much as I can. That may take time, and, of course, it might turn out to be impossible to get word out to you."

"So what do we do meanwhile?" Reetal asked. "If we start lining up our attack group immediately, and then there's no action for another five or six hours, there's always the chance of a leak, with around twenty people in the know."

"And if there's a leak," Quillan agreed, "we've probably had it. No, you'd better wait with that! If I'm not out, and you haven't heard from me before the *Camelot's* actually due to dock, Heraga can still take the group — everyone but yourself — in as scheduled."

"Why everyone but me?" Reetal asked.

"If nothing else works, you might find some way of getting a warning to the liner's security force after they've docked. It isn't much of a possibility, but we can't afford to throw it away."

"Yes, I see." Reetal looked reflective. "What do you think, Heraga?"

The little man shrugged. "You told me that Mr. Quillan is not inexperienced in dealing with, ah, his enemies. If he feels he might accomplish something in the Executive Block, I'm in favor of the plan. The situation certainly could hardly become worse."

"That's the spirit!" Quillan said. "The positive out-
look — that's what a thing like this mainly takes. Can you
arrange for the diner and the uniform?"

"Oh, yes," Heraga said. "I've had myself put in charge of
that detail, naturally."

"Then what can you tell me about the Executive Block's
layout?"

Reetal stood up. "Come over to the desk," she said.
"We've got diagrams."

"The five levels, as you see," Heraga was explaining a
few moments later, "are built directly into the curve
of the Star's shells. Level Five, on the top, is therefore quite
small. The other levels are fairly extensive. Two, Three, and
Four could each accommodate a hundred men comfortably. These levels contain mainly living quarters, private offices, and the like. The Brotherhood men appear to be
occupying the fourth level; Velladon's group the second.
The third may be reserved for meetings between represen-
tatives of the two groups. All three of these levels are connected by single-exit portals to the large entrance area on
the ground level.

"The portals stood open when I went in earlier today,
and there were about twenty armed men lounging about the
entrance hall. I recognized approximately half of them as
being members of the Star's security force. The others were
unfamiliar." Heraga cleared his throat. "There is a possibility that the two groups do not entirely trust each other."

Quillan nodded. "If they're playing around with something like sixty million CR, anybody would have to be crazy
to trust the Brotherhood of Beldon. The transmitter room

98

and the control offices are guarded, too?"

"Yes, but not heavily," Heraga said. "There seem to be only a few men stationed at each of those points. Ostensibly, they're there as a safeguard — in case the imaginary raiders attempt to break out of the subspace section."

"What's the arrangement of the ordinary walk-in tube portals in the Executive Block?"

"There is one which interconnects the five levels. On each of the lower levels there are, in addition, several portals which lead out to various points in the Seventh Star Hotel. On the fifth level, there is only one portal of this kind. Except for the portal which operates between the different levels in the Executive Block, all of them have been rendered unusable at present."

"Unusable in what way?"

"They have been sealed off on the Executive Block side."

"Can you get me a diagram of the entry and exit systems those outgoing portals connect with?" Quillan asked. "I might turn one of them usable again."

"Yes, I can do that."

"How about the communication possibilities?"

"The ComWeb system is functioning normally on the second, third, and fourth levels. It has been shut off on the first level — to avoid the spread of `alarming rumors' by office personnel. There is no ComWeb on the fifth level."

Reetal said, "We'll shift our operating headquarters back to my registered suite then. The ComWebs are turned off in these vacant sections. I'll stay in the other suite in case you find a chance to signal in."

Heraga left a few minutes later to make his arrangements. Reetal smiled at Quillan, a little dubiously.

"Good luck, guy," she said. "Anything else to settle before you start off?"

Quillan nodded. "Couple of details. If you're going to be in your regular suite, and Fluel finds himself with some idle time on hand, he might show up for the dalliance you mentioned."

Reetal's smile changed slightly. Her left hand fluffed the hair at the back of her head, flicked down again. There was a tiny click, and Quillan looked at a small jeweled hair-clasp in her palm, its needle beak pointing at him.

"It hasn't got much range," Reetal said, "but within ten feet it will scramble the Duke's brains just as thoroughly as they need to be scrambled."

"Good enough," Quillan said. "Just don't give that boy the ghost of a chance, doll. He has a rep for playing very unnice games with the ladies."

"I know his reputation." Reetal replaced the tiny gun in her hair. "Anything else?"

"Yes. Let's look in on the Kinmarten girl for a moment. If she's awake, she may have remembered something or other by now that she didn't think to tell you."

They found Solvey Kinmarten awake, and tearfully glad to see Reetal. Quillan was introduced as a member of the legal profession who would do what he could for Solvey and her husband. Solvey frowned prettily, trying very hard to remember anything that might be of use. But it appeared that she had told Reetal all she knew.

2

The blue and white Phalagon House diner, driven by Heraga, was admitted without comment into the Executive Block. It floated on unchallenged through the big entry hall and into a corridor. Immediately behind the first turn of the corridor, the diner paused a few seconds. Its side door opened and closed. The diner moved on.

Quillan, coatless and with the well-worn butt of a big Miam Devil Special protruding from the holster on his right hip, came briskly back along the corridor. Between fifteen and twenty men, their guns also conspicuously in evidence, were scattered about the entrance hall, expressions and attitudes indicating a curious mixture of boredom and uneasy tension. The eyes of about half of them swiveled around to Quillan when he came into the hall; then, with one exception, they looked indifferently away again.

The exception, leaning against the wall near the three open portals to the upper levels, continued to stare as Quillan came toward him, forehead creased in a deep scowl as if he were painfully ransacking his mind for something. Quillan stopped in front of him.

"Chum," he asked, "any idea where Movaine is at the moment? They just give me this message for him —"

Still scowling, the other scratched his chin and blinked. "Uh . . . dunno for sure," he said after a moment. "He oughta be in the third level conference room with the rest of 'em. Uh . . . dunno you oughta barge in there right now, pal! The commodore's *reee-lly* hot about somethin'!"

Quillan looked worried. "Gotta chance it, I guess! Message is pretty important, they say — " He turned, went through the center portal of the three, abruptly found himself walking along a wide, well-lit hall.

Nobody in sight here, or in the first intersecting passage he came to. When he reached the next passage he heard voices on the right, turned toward them, went by a string of closed doors on both sides until, forty feet on, the passage angled again and opened into a long, high-ceilinged room.

The voices came through an open door on the right side of the room. Standing against the wall beside the door were two men whose heads turned sharply toward Quillan as he appeared in the passage. The short, chunky one scowled. The big man next to him, the top of whose head had been permanently seared clear of hair years before by a near miss from a blaster, dropped his jaw slowly. His eyes popped.

"My God!" he said.

"Movaine in there, Baldy?" Quillan inquired, coming up.

"Movaine! He . . . you . . . how —"

The chunky man took out his gun, waved it negligently at Quillan. "Tell the ape to blow, Perk. He isn't wanted here."

"Ape?" Quillan asked softly. His right hand moved, had the gun by the barrel, twisted, reversed the gun, jammed it back with some violence into the chunky man's stomach. "Ape?" he repeated. The chunky man went white.

"Bad News — " Baldy Perk breathed. "Take it easy! That's Orca. He's the commodore's torpedo. How —"

"Where's Movaine?"

"Movaine . . . he . . . uh —"

"All right, he's not here. And Lancion can't have arrived yet. Is Cooms in there?"

"Yeah," Baldy Perk said weakly. "Cooms is in there, Quillan."

"Let's go in." Quillan withdrew the gun, slid it into a pocket, smiled down at Orca. "Get it back from your boss, slob. Be seeing you!"

Orca's voice was a husky whisper.

"You will, friend! You will!"

*   *   *

The conference room was big and sparsely furnished. Four men sat at the long table in its center. Quillan knew two of them — Marras Cooms, second in command of the Beldon Brotherhood's detachment here, and the Duke of Fluel, Movaine's personal gun. Going by Heraga's descriptions, the big, florid-faced man with white hair and flowing white mustaches who was doing the talking was Velladon, the commodore; while the fourth man, younger, wiry, with thinning black hair plastered back across his skull, would be Ryter, chief of the Star's security force.

"What I object to primarily is that the attempt was made without obtaining my consent, and secretly," Velladon was saying, with a toothy grin but in a voice that shook with open fury. "And now it's been made and bungled, you have a damn nerve asking for our help. The problem is yours — and you better take care of it fast! I can't spare Ryter. If —"

"Cooms," Baldy Perk broke in desperately from the door, "Bad News Quillan's here an' —"

The heads of the four men at the table came around simultaneously. The eyes of two of them widened for an instant. Then Marras Cooms began laughing softly.

"Now everything's happened!" he said.

"Cooms," the commodore said testily, "I prefer not to be interrupted. Now —"

"Can't be helped, commodore," Quillan said, moving forward, Perk shuffling along unhappily beside him. "I've got news for Movaine, and the news can't wait."

"Movaine?" the commodore repeated, blue eyes bulging at Quillan. "Movaine! Cooms, who *is* this man?"

"You're looking at Bad News Quillan," Cooms said. "A hijacking specialist, with somewhat numerous sidelines. But the point right now is that he isn't a member of the Brotherhood."

"What!" Velladon's big fist smashed down on the table. *"Now* what kind of a game . . . how did he get *in* here?"

"Well," Quillan said mildly, "I oozed in through the north wall about a minute ago. I —"

He checked, conscious of having created some kind of sensation. The four men at the table were staring up at him without moving. Baldy Perk appeared to be holding his breath. Then the commodore coughed, cleared his throat, drummed his fingers on the table.

He said reflectively: "He could have news — good or bad — at that! For all of us." He chewed on one of his mustache tips, grinned suddenly up at Quillan. "Well, sit down, friend! Let's talk. You can't talk to Movaine, you see. Movaine's, um, had an accident. Passed away suddenly half an hour ago."

"Sorry to hear it," Quillan said. "That's the sort of thing that happens so often in the Brotherhood." He swung a chair around, sat down facing the table. "You're looking well tonight, Fluel," he observed.

The Duke of Fluel, lean and dapper in silver jacket and tight-fitting silver trousers, gave him a wintry smile, said nothing.

"Now, then, friend," Velladon inquired confidentially, "just what was your business with Movaine?"

"Well, it will come to around twenty per cent of the take," Quillan informed him. "We won't argue about a half-million CR more or less. But around twenty per."

The faces turned thoughtful. After some seconds, the commodore asked, "And who's we?"

"A number of citizens," Quillan said, "who have been rather unhappy since discovering that you, too, are interested in Lady Pendrake and her pals. We'd gone to considerable expense and trouble to . . . well, her ladyship was scheduled to show up in Mezmiali, you know. And now she isn't going to show up there. All right, that's business. Twenty per — no hard feelings. Otherwise, it won't do you a bit of good to blow up the Star and the liner. There'd still be loose talk — maybe other complications, too. You know how it goes. You wouldn't be happy, and neither would Yaco. Right?"

The commodore's massive head turned back to Cooms. "How well do you know this man, Marras?"

Cooms grinned dryly. "Well enough."

"Is he leveling?"

"He'd be nuts to be here if he wasn't. And he isn't nuts — at least, not that way."

"There might be a question about that," Fluel observed. He looked at the commodore. "Why not ask him for a couple of the names that are in it with him?"

"Hagready and Boltan," Quillan said.

Velladon chewed the other mustache rip. "I know Hagready. If he —"

"I know both of them," Cooms said. "Boltan works hijacking crews out of Orado. Quillan operates there occasionally."

"Pappy Boltan's an old business associate," Quillan said. "Reliable sort of a guy. Doesn't mind taking a few chances either."

Velladon's protruding blue eyes measured him a moment. "We can check on those two, you know —"

"Check away," Quillan said.

Velladon nodded. "We will." He was silent for a second or two, then glanced over at Cooms. "There've been no leaks on our side," he said. "And they must have known about this for weeks! Of all the inept, bungling —"

"Ah, don't be too hard on the Brotherhood, commodore," Quillan said. "Leaks happen. You ought to know."

"What do you mean?" Velladon snapped.

"From what we heard, the Brotherhood's pulling you out of a hole here. You should feel rather kindly toward them."

The commodore stared at him reflectively. Then he grinned. "Could be I should," he said. "Did you come here alone?"

"Yes."

The commodore nodded. "If you're bluffing, God help you. If you're not, your group's in. Twenty per. No time for haggling — we can raise Yaco's price to cover it." He stood up, and Ryter stood up with him. "Marras," the commodore went on, "tell him what's happened. If he's half as hot as he sounds, he's the boy to put on that job. Let him get in on a little of the work for the twenty per cent. Ryter, come on. We —"

"One moment, sir," Quillan interrupted. He took Orca's gun by the muzzle from his pocket, held it out to Velladon. "One of your men lost this thing. The one outside the door. If you don't mind — he might pout if he doesn't get it back."

The fifth level of the Executive Block appeared to be, as Heraga had said, quite small. The tiny entry hall, on which two walk-in portals opened, led directly into the large room where the two Pendrake rest cubicles had been placed. One of the cubicles now stood open. To right and left, a narrow passage stretched away from the room, ending apparently in smaller rooms.

Baldy Perk was perspiring profusely.

"Now right here," he said in a low voice, "was where I was standing. Movaine was over there, on the right of the cubicle, and Cooms was beside him. Rubero was a little behind me, hanging on to the punk — that Kinmarten. An' the Duke" — he nodded back at the wide doorspace to the hall — "was standing back there."

"All right. The punk's opened the cubicle a crack, looking like he's about to pass out while he's doin' it. This bearded guy, Eltak, stands in front of the cubicle, holding the gadget he controls the thing with —"

"Where's the gadget now?" Quillan asked.

"Marras Cooms' got it."

"How does it work?"

Baldy shook his head. "We can't figure it out. It's got all kinds of little knobs and dials on it. Push this one an' it squeaks, turn that one an' it buzzes. Like that."

Quillan nodded. "All right. What happened?"

"Well, Movaine tells the old guy to go ahead an' do the demonstrating. The old guy sort of grins and fiddles with the gadget. The cubicle door pops open an' this thing comes pouring out. I never seen nothin' like it! It's like a barn door with dirty fur on it! It swirls up an' around an' — it wraps its upper end clean around poor Movaine. He never even screeches."

"Then everything pops at once. The old guy is laughing like crazy, an' that half-smart Rubero drills him right through the head. I take one shot at the thing, low so's not to hit Movaine, an' then we're all running. I'm halfway to the hall when Cooms tears past me like a rocket. The Duke an' the others are already piling out through the portal. I get to the hall, and there's this terrific smack of sound in the room. I look back . . . an' . . . an' — " Baldy paused and gulped.

"And what?" Quillan asked.

"There, behind the cubicles, I see poor Movaine stickin' halfway out o' the wall!" Baldy reported in a hushed whisper.

"*Half*way out of the wall?"

"From the waist up he's in it! From the waist down he's dangling into the room! I tell you, I never seen nothin' like it."

"And this Hlat creature —"

"That's gone. I figure the smack I heard was when it hit the wall flat, carrying Movaine. It went on into it. Movaine didn't — at least, the last half of him didn't."

"Well," Quillan said after a pause, "in a way, Movaine got his demonstration. The Hlats can move through solid matter and carry other objects along with them, as advertised. If Yaco can work out how it's done and build a gadget that does the same thing, they're getting the Hlats cheap. What happened then?"

"I told Marras Cooms about Movaine, and he sent me and a half dozen other boys back up here with riot guns to see what we could do for him. Which was nothin', of course." Baldy gulped again. "We finally cut this end of him off with a beam and took it back down."

"The thing didn't show up while you were here?"

Baldy shuddered and said, "Naw."

"And the technician . . . was dead?"

"Sure. Hole in his head you could shove your fist through."

"Somebody," Quillan observed, "ought to drill Rubero for that stupid trick!"

"The Duke did — first thing after we got back to the fourth level."

"So the Hlat's on the loose, and all we really have at the moment are the cubicles . . . and Rest Warden Kinmarten.

Where's he, by the way?"

"He tried to take off when we got down to Level Four, an' somebody cold-cocked him. The doc says he ought to be coming around again pretty soon."

Quillan grunted, shoved the Miam Devil Special into its holster, said, "O.K., you stay here where you can watch the room and those passages and the hall. If you feel the floor start moving under you, scream. I'll take a look at the cubicle."

Lady Pendrake's cubicle was about half as big again as a standard one; but, aside from one detail, its outer settings, instruments, and operating devices appeared normal. The modification was a recess almost six feet long and a foot wide and deep, in one side, which could be opened either to the room or to the interior of the rest cubicle, but not simultaneously to both. Quillan already knew his purpose; the supposed other cubicle was a camouflaged food locker, containing fifty-pound slabs of sea beef, each of which represented a meal for the Hlat. The recess made it possible to feed it without allowing it to be seen, or, possibly, attempting to emerge. Kinmarten's nervousness, as reported by his wife, seemed understandable. Any rest warden might get disturbed over such a charge.

Quillan asked over his shoulder, "Anyone find out yet why the things can't get out of a closed rest cubicle?"

"Yeah," Baldy Perk said. "Kinmarten says it's the cubicle's defense fields. They could get through the material. They can't get through the field."

"Someone think to energize the Executive Block's battle fields?" Quillan inquired.

"Yeah. Velladon took care of that before he came

screaming up to the third level to argue with Cooms and Fluel."

"So it can't slip out of the Block unless it shows itself down on the ground level when the entry lock's open."

"Yeah," Baldy muttered. "But I dunno. Is that good?"

Quillan looked at him. "Well, we *would* like it back."

"Why? There's fifty more coming in on the liner to-night"

"We don't have the fifty yet. If someone louses up that detail —"

"Yawk!" Baldy said faintly. There was a crash of sound as his riot gun went off. Quillan spun about, hair bristling, gun out. "What happened?"

"I'll swear," Baldy said, white-faced, "I saw something moving along that passage!"

Quillan looked, saw nothing, slowly replaced the gun. "Baldy," he said, "if you think you see it again, just say so. That's an order! If it comes at us, we get out of this level fast. But we don't shoot before we have to. If we kill it, it's no good to us. Got that?"

"Yeah," Baldy said. "But I got an idea now, Bad News." He nodded at the other cubicle. "Let's leave that meat box open."

"Why?"

"If it's hungry," Baldy explained simply, "I'd sooner it wrapped itself around a few chunks of sea beef, an' not around me."

Quillan punched him encouragingly in the shoulder. "Baldy," he said, "in your own way, you *have* had an idea! But we won't leave the meat box open. When Kinmarten wakes up, I want him to show me how to bait this cubicle with a piece of sea beef, so it'll snap shut if the Hlat goes inside. Meanwhile it won't hurt if it gets a little hungry."

"That," said Baldy, "isn't the way I feel about it."

"There must be around a hundred and fifty people in the Executive Block at present," Quillan said. "Look at it that way! Even if the thing keeps stuffing away, your odds are pretty good, Baldy."

Baldy shuddered.

Aside from a dark bruise high on his forehead, Brock Kinmarten showed no direct effects of having been knocked out. However, his face was strained and his voice not entirely steady. It was obvious that the young rest warden had never been in a similarly unnerving situation before. But he was making a valiant effort not to appear frightened and, at the same time, to indicate that he would co-operate to the best of his ability with his captors.

He'd regained consciousness by the time Quillan and Perk returned to the fourth level, and Quillan suggested bringing him to Marras Cooms' private quarters for questioning. The Brotherhood chief agreed; he was primarily interested in finding out how the Hlat-control device functioned.

Kinmarten shook his head. He knew nothing about the instrument, he said, except that it was called a Hlat-talker. It was very unfortunate that Eltak had been shot, because Eltak undoubtedly could have told them all they wanted to know about it. If what he had told Kinmarten was true, Eltak had been directly involved in the development of the device.

"Was he some Federation scientist?" Cooms asked, fiddling absently with the mysterious cylindrical object.

"No, sir," the young man said. "But — again if what he told me was the truth — he was the man who actually discovered these Hlats. At least, he was the first man to discover them who wasn't immediately killed by them."

Cooms glanced thoughtfully at Quillan, then asked, "And where was that?"

Kinmarten shook his head again. "He didn't tell me. And I didn't really want to know. I was anxious to get our convoy to its destination, and then to be relieved of the assignment. I . . . well, I've been trained to act as Rest Warden to human beings, after all, not to monstrosities!" He produced an uncertain smile, glancing from one to the other of his interrogators. The smile promptly faded out again.

"You've no idea at all then about the place they came from?" Cooms asked expressionlessly.

"Oh, yes," Kinmarten said hastily. "Eltak talked a great deal about the Hlats, and actually — except for its location — gave me a fairly good picture of what the planet must be like. For one thing, it's an uncolonized world, of course. It must be terratype or very nearly so, because Eltak lived there for fifteen years with apparently only a minimum of equipment. The Hlats are confined to a single large island. He discovered them by accident and —"

"What was he doing there?"

"Well, sir, he came from Hyles-Frisian. He was a crim . . . he'd been engaged in some form of piracy, and when the authorities began looking for him, he decided it would be best to get clean out of the Hub. He cracked up his ship on this world and couldn't leave again. When he discovered the Hlats and realized their peculiar ability, he kept out of their way and observed them. He found out they had a means of communicating with each other, and that he could duplicate it. That stopped them from harming him, and eventually, he said, he was using them like hunting dogs.

They were accustomed to co-operating with one another, because when there was some animal around that was too large for one of them to handle, they would attack it in a group . . ."

He went on for another minute or two on the subject. The Hlats — the word meant "rock lion" in one of the Hyles-Frisian dialects, describing a carnivorous animal which had some superficial resemblance to the creatures Eltak had happened on — frequented the seacoast and submerged themselves in sand, rocks and debris, whipping up out of it to seize some food animal, and taking it down with them again to devour it at leisure.

Quillan interrupted, "You heard what happened to the man it attacked on the fifth level?"

"Yes, sir."

"Why would the thing have left him half outside the wall as it did?"

Kinmarten said that it must simply have been moving too fast. It could slip into and out of solid substances without a pause itself, but it needed a little time to restructure an object it was carrying in the same manner. No more time, however, than two or three seconds — depending more on the nature of the object than on its size, according to Eltak.

"It can restructure *anything* in that manner?" Quillan asked.

Kinmarten hesitated. "Well, sir, I don't know. I suppose there might be limitations on its ability. Eltak told me the one we were escorting had been the subject of extensive experimentation during the past year, and that the results are very satisfactory."

"Suppose it carries a living man through a wall. Will the man still be alive when he comes out on the other side, assuming the Hlat doesn't kill him deliberately?"

"Yes, sir. The process itself wouldn't hurt him."

Quillan glanced at Cooms. "You know," he said, "we might be letting Yaco off too cheaply!"

Cooms raised an eyebrow warningly, and Quillan grinned. "Our friend will be learning about Yaco soon enough. Why did Eltak tell the creature to attack, Kinmarten?"

"Sir, I don't know," Kinmarten said. "He was a man of rather violent habits. My impression, however, was that he was simply attempting to obtain a hostage."

"How did he get off that island with the Hlat?"

"A University League explorer was investigating the planet. Eltak contacted them and obtained the guarantee of a full pardon and a large cash settlement in return for what he could tell them about the Hlats. They took him and this one specimen along for experimentation."

"What about the Hlats on the *Camelot*?"

"Eltak said those had been quite recently trapped on the island."

Cooms ran his fingers over the cylinder, producing a rapid series of squeaks and whistles. "That's one thing Yaco may not like," he observed. "They won't have a monopoly on the thing."

Quillan shook his head. "Their scientists don't have to work through red tape like the U-League. By the time the news breaks — if the Federation ever intends to break it — Yaco will have at least a five-year start on everyone else. That's all an outfit like that needs." He looked at Kinmarten. "Any little thing you haven't thought to tell us, friend?" he inquired pleasantly.

A thin film of sweat showed suddenly on Kinmarten's

forehead.

"No, sir," he said. "I've really told you everything I know. I —"

"Might try him under dope," Cooms said absently.

"Uh-uh!" Quillan said. "I want him wide awake to help me bait the cubicle for the thing. Has Velladon shown any indication of becoming willing to co-operate in hunting it?"

Cooms gestured with his head. "Ask Fluel! I sent him down to try to patch things up with the commodore. He just showed up again."

Quillan glanced around. The Duke was lounging in the doorway. He grinned slightly, said, "Velladon's still sore at us. But he'll talk to Quillan. Kinmarten here . . . did he tell you his wife's on the Star?"

Brock Kinmarten went utterly white. Cooms looked at him, said softly, "No, that must have slipped his mind."

Fluel said, "Yeah. Well, she is. And Ryter says they'll have her picked up inside half an hour. When they bring her in, we really should check on how candid Kinmarten's been about everything."

The rest warden said in a voice that shook uncontrollably, "Gentlemen, my wife knows absolutely nothing about these matters! I swear it! She —"

Quillan stood up. "Well, I'll go see if I can't get Velladon in a better mood. Are you keeping that Hlat-talker, Cooms?"

Cooms smiled. "I am."

"Marras figures," the Duke's flat voice explained, "that if the thing comes into the room and he squeaks at it a few times, he won't get hurt."

"That's possible," Cooms said, un-ruffled. "At any rate, I intend to hang on to it."

"Well, I wouldn't play around with those buttons too much," Quillan observed.

"Why not?"

"You might get lucky and tap out some pattern that spells `Come to chow' in the Hlat's vocabulary."

3

There were considerably more men in evidence on Level Two than on the fourth, and fewer signs of nervousness. The Star men had been told of the Hlat's escape from its cubicle, but weren't taking it too seriously. Quillan was conducted to the commodore and favored with an alarmingly toothy grin. Ryter, the security chief, joined them a few seconds later. Apparently, Velladon had summoned him.

Velladon said, "Ryter here's made a few transmitter calls. We hear Pappy Boltan pulled his outfit out of the Orado area about a month ago. Present whereabouts unknown. Hagready went off on some hush-hush job at around the same time."

Quillan smiled. "Uh-huh! So he did."

"We also," said Ryter, "learned a number of things about you personally." He produced a thin smile. "You lead a busy and — apparently — profitable life."

"Business is fair," Quillan agreed. "But it can always be improved."

The commodore turned on the toothy grin. "So all right," he growled, "you're clear. We rather liked what we learned. Eh, Ryter?"

Ryter nodded.

"This Brotherhood of Beldon, now — " The commodore shook his head heavily.

Quillan was silent a moment. "They might be getting sloppy," he said. "I don't know. It's one possibility. They used to be a rather sharp outfit, you know."

"That's what I'd heard!" Velladon chewed savagely on his mustache, asked finally, "What's another possibility?"

Quillan leaned back in his chair. "Just a feeling, so far. But the business with the cubicle upstairs might have angles that weren't mentioned."

They looked at him thoughtfully. Ryter said, "Mind amplifying that?"

"Cooms told me," Quillan said, "that Nome Lancion had given Movaine instructions to make a test with Lady Pendrake on the quiet and find out if those creatures actually can do what they're supposed to do. I think he was telling the truth. Nome tends to be overcautious when it's a really big deal. Unless he's sure of the Hlats, he wouldn't want to be involved in a thing like blowing up the Star and the liner."

The commodore scowled absently. "Uh-huh," he said. "He knows we can't back out of it —"

"All right. The Brotherhood's full of ambitious men. Behind Lancion, Movaine was top man. Cooms behind him; Fluel behind Cooms. Suppose that Hlat-control device Cooms is hanging on to so tightly isn't as entirely incomprehensible as they make it out to be. Suppose Cooms makes a deal with Eltak. Eltak tickles the gadget, and the Hlat kills Movaine. Rubero immediately guns down Eltak — and is killed by Fluel a couple of minutes later, supposedly for blowing his top and killing the man who knew how to control the Hlat."

Ryter cleared his throat. "Fluel was Movaine's gun," he observed.

"So he was," Quillan said. "Would you like the Duke to be yours?"

Ryter grinned, shook his head. "No, thanks!"

Quillan looked back at Velladon. "How well are you actually covered against the Brotherhood?"

"Well, *that's* air-tight," the commodore said. "We've got `em outgunned here. When the liner lands, we'll be about even. But Lancion won't start anything. We're *too* even. Once we're clear of the Star, we don't meet again. We deal with Yaco individually. The Brotherhood has the Hlats, and we have the trained Federation technicians accompanying them, who . . . who —"

"Who alone are supposed to be able to inform Yaco how to control the Hlats," Ryter finished for him. The security chief's face was expressionless.

"By God!" the commodore said softly.

"Well, it's only a possibility that somebody's playing dirty," Quillan remarked. "We'd want to be sure of it. But if anyone can handle a Hlat with that control instrument, the Brotherhood has an advantage now that it isn't talking about — it can offer Yaco everything Yaco needs in one package. Of course, Yaco might still be willing to pay for the Hlat technicians. If it didn't, you and Ryter could make the same kind of trouble for it that my friends can."

The color was draining slowly from Velladon's face. "There's a difference," he said. "If we threaten to make trouble for Yaco, they'd see to it that our present employers learn that Ryter and I are still alive"

"That's the Mooleys, eh?"

"Yes."

"Tough." Quillan knuckled his chin thoughtfully. "Well, let's put it this way then," he said. "My group doesn't have *that* kind of problem, but if things worked out so that we'd have something more substantial than nuisance value to offer Yaco, we'd prefer it, of course."

Velladon nodded. "Very understandable! Under the circumstances co-operation appears to be indicated, eh?"

"That's what I had in mind."

"You've made a deal," Velladon said. "Any immediate suggestions?"

Quillan looked at his watch. "A couple. We don't want to make any mistake about this. It's still almost five hours before the *Camelot* pulls in, and until she does you're way ahead on firepower. I wouldn't make any accusations just now. But you might mention to Cooms you'd like to borrow the Hlat gadget to have it examined by some of your technical experts. The way he reacts might tell us something. If he balks, the matter shouldn't be pushed too hard at the moment — it's a tossup whether you or the Brotherhood has a better claim to the thing."

"But then there's Kinmarten, the rest warden in charge of the cubicle. I talked with him while Cooms and Fluel were around, but he may have been briefed on what to say. Cooms mentioned doping him, which could be a convenient way of keeping him shut up, assuming he knows more than he's told. He's one of the personnel you're to offer Yaco. I think you can insist on having Kinmarten handed over to you immediately. It should be interesting again to see how Cooms reacts."

Velladon's big head nodded vigorously. "Good idea!"

"By the way," Quillan said, "Fluel mentioned you've been looking for Kinmarten's wife, the second rest warden on the Pendrake convoy. Found her yet?"

"Not a trace, so far," Ryter said.

"That's a little surprising, too, isn't it?"

"Under the circumstances," the commodore said, "it might not be surprising at all!" He had regained his color, was beginning to look angry. "If they —"

"Well," Quillan said soothingly, "we don't *know*. It's just that things do seem to be adding up a little. Now, there's one other point. We should do something immediately about catching that Hlat."

Velladon grunted and picked at his teeth with his thumbnail. "It would be best to get it back in its cubicle, of course. But I'm not worrying about it — just an animal, after all. Even the light hardware those Beldon fancy Dans carry should handle it. You use a man-sized gun, I see. So do I. If it shows up around here, it gets smeared, that's all. There're fifty more of the beasts on the *Camelot*."

Quillan nodded. "You're right on that. But there's the possibility that it is being controlled by the Brotherhood at present. If it is, it isn't just an animal any more. It could be turned into a thoroughly dangerous nuisance."

The commodore thought a moment, nodded. "You're right, I suppose. What do you want to do about it?"

"Baiting the cubicle on the fifth level might work. Then there should be life-detectors in the Star's security supplies —"

Ryter nodded. "We have a couple of dozen of them, but not in the Executive Block. They were left in the security building."

The commodore stood up. "You stay here with Ryter," he told Quillan. "There're a couple of other things I want to go over with you two. I'll order the life-detectors from the office here — second passage down, isn't it, Ryter? . . . And, Ryter, I have another idea. I'm pulling the man in space-armor off the subspace portal and detailing him to Level Five." He grinned at Quillan. "That boy's got a brace of grenades and built-in spray guns! If Cooms is thinking of pulling any funny stunts up there, he'll think again."

*   *   *

The commodore headed briskly down the narrow passageway, his big holstered gun slapping his thigh with every step. The two security guards stationed at the door to the second level office came to attention as he approached, saluted smartly. He grunted, went in without returning the salutes, and started over toward the ComWeb on a desk at the far end of the big room, skirting the long, dusty-looking black rug beside one wall.

Velladon unbuckled his gun belt, placed the gun on the desk, sat down and switched on the ComWeb.

Behind him, the black rug stirred silently and rose up.

"You called that one," Ryter was saying seven or eight minutes later, "almost too well!"

Quillan shook his head, poked at the commodore's gun on the desk with his finger, looked about the silent office and back at the door where a small group of security men stood staring in at them.

"Three men gone without a sound!" he said. He indicated the glowing disk of the ComWeb. "He had time enough to turn it on, not time enough to make his call. Any chance of camouflaged portals in this section?"

"No," Ryter said. "I know the location of every portal in the Executive Block. No number of men could have taken Velladon and the two guards without a fight anyway. We'd have heard it. It didn't happen that way."

"Which leaves," Quillan said, "one way it could have happened." He jerked his head toward the door. "Will those men keep quiet?"

"If I tell them to."

"Then play it like this. Two guards have vanished. The Hlat obviously did it. The thing's deadly. That'll keep every man in the group on the alert every instant from now on. But we don't say Velladon has vanished. He's outside in the Star at the moment, taking care of something"

Ryter licked his lips. "What does that buy us?"

"If the Brotherhood's responsible for this —"

"I don't take much stock in coincidences," Ryter said.

"Neither do I. But the Hlat's an animal; it can't tell them it's carried out the job. If they don't realize we suspect them, it gives us some advantage. For the moment, we just carry on as planned, and get rid of the Hlat in one way or another as the first step. The thing's three times as dangerous as any-one suspected — except, apparently, the Brotherhood. Get the life-detectors over here as soon as you can, and slap a space-armor guard on the fifth level."

Ryter hesitated, nodded. "All right."

"Another thing," Quillan said, "Cooms may have the old trick in mind of working from the top down. If he can take you out along with a few other key men, he might have this outfit demoralized to the point of making up for the differ-ence in the number of guns — especially if the Hlat's still on his team. You'd better keep a handful of the best boys you have around here glued to your back from now on."

Ryter smiled bleakly. "Don't worry. I intend to. What about you?"

"I don't think they're planning on giving me any per-sonal attention at the moment. My organization is outside, not here. And it would look odd to the Brotherhood if I started dragging a few Star guards around with me at this point."

Ryter shrugged. "Suit yourself. It's your funeral if you've guessed wrong."

*   *   *

"There was nothing," Quillan told Marras Cooms, "that you could actually put a finger on. It was just that I got a very definite impression that the commodore and Ryter may have something up their sleeves. Velladon's looking too self-satisfied to suit me."

The Brotherhood chief gnawed his lower lip reflectively. He seemed thoughtful, not too disturbed. Cooms might be thoroughly afraid of the escaped Hlat, but he wouldn't have reached his present position in Nome Lancion's organization if he had been easily frightened by what other men were planning.

He said, "I warned Movaine that if Velladon learned we'd checked out the Hlat, he wasn't going to like it."

"He doesn't," Quillan said. "He regards it as something pretty close to an attempted double cross."

Cooms grinned briefly. "It was."

"Of course. The question is, what can he do about it? He's got you outgunned two to one, but if he's thinking of jumping you before Lancion gets here, he stands to lose more men than he can afford to without endangering the entire operation for himself."

Cooms was silent a few seconds. "There's an unpleasant possibility which didn't occur to me until a short while ago," he said then. "The fact is that Velladon actually may have us outgunned here by something like four to one. If that's the case, he can afford to lose quite a few men. In fact, he'd prefer to."

Quillan frowned. "*Four* to one? How's that?"

Cooms said, "The commodore told us he intended to let only around half of the Seventh Star's security force in on the Hlat deal. The other half was supposed to have been dumped out of one of the subspace section's locks early today, without benefit of suits. We had no reason to disbelieve him. Velladon naturally would want to cut down the number of men who got in on the split with him to as many as he actually needed. But if he's been thinking about eliminating us from the game, those other men may still be alive and armed."

Quillan grunted. "I see. You know, that could explain something that looked a little odd to me."

"What was that?" Cooms asked.

Quillan said, "After they discovered down there that two of their guards were missing and decided the Hlat must have been on their level, I tried to get hold of the commodore again. Ryter told me Velladon won't be available for a while, that he's outside in the Star, taking care of something there. I wondered what could be important enough to get Velladon to leave the Executive Block at present, but —"

"Brother, I'm way ahead of you!" Cooms said. His expression hardened. "That doesn't look good. But at least he can't bring in reinforcements without tipping us off. We've got our own guards down with theirs at the entrance."

Quillan gave him a glance, then nodded at the wall beyond them. "That's a portal over there, Marras. How many of them on this level?"

"Three or four. Why? The outportals have been plugged, man! Sealed off. Fluel checked them over when we moved in."

"Sure they're sealed." Quillan stood up, went to the portal, stood looking at the panel beside it a moment, then pressed on it here and there, and removed it. "Come over here, friend. I suppose portal work's been out of your line. I'll show you how fast a thing like that can get *un*-plugged!"

He slid a pocketbook-sized tool kit out of his belt, snapped it open. About a minute later, the lifeless VACANT sign above the portal flickered twice, then acquired a steady white glow.

"Portal in operation," Quillan announced. "I'll seal it off again now. But that should give you the idea."

Cooms' tongue flicked over his lips. "Could somebody portal through to this level from the Star while the exits are sealed here?"

"If the mechanisms have been set for that purpose, the portals can be opened again at any time from the Star side. The Duke's an engineer of sorts. isn't he? Let him check on it. He should have been thinking of the point himself, as far as that goes. Anyway, Velladon can bring in as many men as he likes to his own level without using the main entrance." He considered. "I didn't see anything to indicate that he's started doing it —"

Marras Cooms shrugged irritably. "That means nothing! It would be easy enough to keep half a hundred men hidden away on any of the lower levels."

"I suppose that's right. Well, if the commodore intends to play rough, you should have some warning anyway."

"What kind of warning?"

"There's Kinmarten and that Hlat-talking gadget, for example," Quillan pointed out. "Velladon would want both of those in his possession and out of the way where they can't get hurt before he starts any shooting."

Cooms looked at him for a few seconds. "Ryter," he said then, "sent half a dozen men up here for Kinmarten just after you got back! Velladon's supposed to deliver the Hlats' attendants to Yaco, so I let them have Kinmarten." He paused. "They asked for the Hlat-talker, too."

Quillan grunted. "Did you give them that?"

"No."

"Well," Quillan said after a moment, "that doesn't necessarily mean that we're in for trouble with the Star group.

But it does mean, I think, that we'd better stay ready for it!" He stood up. "I'll get back down there and go on with the motions of getting the hunt for the Hlat organized. Velladon would sooner see the thing get caught, too, of course, so he shouldn't try to interfere with that. If I spot anything that looks suspicious, I'll get the word to you."

"I never," said Orca, unconsciously echoing Baldy Perk, "saw anything like it!" The commodore's chunky little gunman was ashen-faced. The circle of Star men standing around him hardly looked happier. Most of them were staring down at the empty lower section of a suit of space armor which appeared to have been separated with a neat diagonal slice from its upper part.

"Let's get it straight," Ryter said, a little unsteadily. "You say this half of the suit was lying against the wall like *that?*"

"Not exactly," Quillan told him. "When we got up to the fifth level the suit was stuck against the wall — like that — about eight feet above the floor. That was in the big room where the cubicles are. When Kinmarten and Orca and I finally got the suit worked away from the wall, I expected frankly that we'd find half the body of the guard still inside. But he'd vanished."

Ryter cleared his throat. "Apparently," he said, "the creature drew the upper section of the suit into the wall by whatever means it uses, then stopped applying the transforming process to the metal, and simply moved on with the upper part of the suit and the man."

Quillan nodded. "That's what it looks like."

"But he had *two grenades!*" Orca burst out. "He had sprayguns! How could it get him that way?"

"Brother," Quillan said, "grenades won't help you much

if you don't spot what's moving up behind you!"

Orca glared speechlessly at him. Ryter said, "All right! We've lost another man. We're not going to lose any more. We'll station no more guards on the fifth level. Now, get everyone who isn't on essential guard duty to the main room, and split `em up into life-detector units. Five men to each detail, one to handle the detector, four to stay with him, guns out. If the thing comes back to this level, we want to have it spotted the instant it arrives. Orca, you stay here — and keep *your* gun out!"

The men filed out hurriedly. Ryter turned to Quillan. "Were you able to get the cubicle baited?"

Quillan nodded. "Kinmarten figured out how the thing should be set for the purpose. If the Hlat goes in after the sea beef, it's trapped. Of course, if the hunting it's been doing was for food, it mightn't be interested in the beef."

"We don't know," Ryter said, "that the hunting it's been doing was for food."

"No. Did you manage to get the control device from Cooms?"

Ryter shook his head. "He's refused to hand it over."

"If you tried to take it from him" Quillan said, "you might have a showdown on your hands."

"And if this keeps on," Ryter said, "I may prefer a showdown! Another few rounds of trouble with the Hlat, and the entire operation could blow up in our faces! The men aren't used to that kind of thing. It's shaken them up. If we've got to take care of the Brotherhood, I'd rather do it while I still have an organized group. Where did you leave Kinmarten, by the way?"

"He's back in that little room with his two guards," Quillan said.

"Well, he should be all right there. We can't spare — "

Ryter's body jerked violently. *"What's that?"*

There had been a single thudding crash somewhere in the level. Then shouts and cursing.

"Main hall!" Quillan said. "Come on!"

The main hall was a jumble of excitedly jabbering Star men when they arrived there. Guns waved about, and the various groups were showing a marked tendency to stand with their backs toward one another and their faces toward the walls.

Ryter's voice rose in a shout that momentarily shut off the hubbub. *"What's going on here?"*

Men turned, hands pointed, voices babbled again. Someone nearby said sharply and distinctly, " . . . Saw it drop right out of the ceiling!" Farther down the hall, another group shifted aside enough to disclose it had been clustered about something which looked a little like the empty shell of a gigantic black beetle.

The missing section of the suit of space armor had been returned. But not its occupant.

Quillan moved back a step, turned, went back down the passage from which they had emerged, pulling the Miam Devil from its holster. Behind him the commotion continued; Ryter was shouting something about getting the life-detector units over there. Quillan went left down the first intersecting corridor, right again on the following one, keeping the gun slightly raised before him. Around the next corner, he saw the man on guard over the portal connecting the building levels facing him, gun pointed.

"What happened?" the guard asked shakily.

Quillan shook his head, coming up. "That thing got another one!"

The guard breathed, "By God!" and lowered his gun a little. Quillan raised his a little, the Miam Devil grunted, and the guard sighed and went down. Quillan went past him along the hall, stopped two doors beyond the portal and rapped on the locked door.

"Quillan here. Open up!"

The door opened a crack, and one of Kinmarten's guards looked out questioningly. Quillan shot him through the head, slammed on into the room across the collapsing body, saw the second guard wheeling toward him, shot again, and slid the gun back into the holster. Kinmarten, standing beside a table six feet away, right hand gripping a heavy marble ashtray, was staring at him in white-faced shock.

"Take it easy, chum!" Quillan said, turning toward him. "I —"

He ducked hurriedly as the ashtray came whirling through the air toward his head. An instant later, a large fist smacked the side of Kinmarten's jaw. The rest warden settled limply to the floor.

"Sorry to do that, pal," Quillan muttered, stooping over him. "Things are rough all over right now." He hauled Kinmarten upright, bent, and had the unconscious young man across his shoulder. The hall was still empty except for the body of the portal guard. Quillan laid Kinmarten on the carpet before the portal, hauled the guard off into the room, and pulled the door to the room shut behind him as he came out. Picking up Kinmarten, he stepped into the portal with him and jabbed the fifth level button. A moment later, he moved out into the small dim entry hall on the fifth level, the gun in his right hand again.

He stood there silently for some seconds, looking about him listening. The baited cubicle yawned widely at him

from the center of the big room. Nothing seemed to be stir-
ring. Kinmarten went back to the floor. Quillan moved over
to the panel which concealed the other portal's mechanisms.

He had the outportal unsealed in considerably less than
a minute this time, and slapped the panel gently back in
place. He turned back to Kinmarten and started to bend
down for him, then straightened quietly again, turning his
head.

Had there been a flicker of shadowy motion just then at
the edge of his vision, behind the big black cube of the Hlat's
food locker? Quillan remained perfectly still, the Miam
Devil ready and every sense straining for an indication that
the thing was there — or approaching stealthily now, gliding
behind the surfaces of floor or ceiling or walls like an under-
water swimmer.

But half a minute passed and nothing else happened. He
went down on one knee beside Kinmarten, the gun still in
his right hand. With his left, he carefully wrestled the rest
warden back up across his shoulder, came upright, moved
three steps to the side, and disappeared in the outportal.

4

Reetal Destone unlocked the entry door to her suite and
stepped hurriedly inside, letting the door slide shut behind her. She crossed the room to the ComWeb stand and
switched on the playback. There was the succession of tin-
kling tones which indicated nothing had been recorded.

She shut the instrument off again, passing her tongue
lightly over her lips. No further messages from Heraga . . .

And none from Quillan.

She shook her head, feeling a surge of sharp anxiety, glanced at her watch and told herself that, after all, less than two hours had passed since Quillan had gone into the Executive Block. Heraga reported there had been no indications of disturbance or excitement when he passed through the big entrance hall on his way out. So Quillan, at any rate, had succeeded in bluffing his way into the upper levels.

It remained a desperate play, at best.

Reetal went down the short passage to her bedroom. As she came into the room, her arms were caught from the side at the elbows, pulled suddenly and painfully together behind her. She stood still, frozen with shock.

"In a hurry, sweetheart?" Fluel's flat voice said.

Reetal managed a breathless giggle. "Duke! You startled me! How did you get in?"

She felt one hand move up her arm to her shoulder. Then she was swung about deftly and irresistibly, held pinned back against the wall, still unable to move her arms.

He looked at her a moment, asked, "Where are you hiding it this time?"

"Hiding what, Duke?"

"I've been told sweet little Reetal always carries a sweet little gun around with her in some shape or form or other."

Reetal shook her head, her eyes widening. "Duke, what's the matter? I . . ."

He let go of her suddenly, and his slap exploded against the side of her face. Reetal cried out, dropping her head between her hands. Immediately he had her wrists again, and her fingers were jerked away from the jeweled ornament in her hair.

"So that's where it is!" Fluel said. "Thought it might be. Don't get funny again now, sweetheart. Just stay quiet."

She stayed quiet, wincing a little as he plucked the glittering little device out of her hair. He turned it around in his fingers, examining it, smiled and slid it into an inside pocket, and took her arm again. "Let's go to the front room, Reetal," he said almost pleasantly. "We've got a few things to do."

A minute later, she was seated sideways on a lounger, her wrists fastened right and left to its armrests. The Duke placed a pocket recorder on the floor beside her. "This is a crowded evening, sweetheart," he remarked, "which is lucky for you in a way. We'll have to rush things along a little. I'll snap the recorder on in a minute so you can answer questions — No, keep quiet. Just listen very closely now, so you'll know what the right answers are. If you get rattled and gum things up, the Duke's going to get annoyed with you."

He sat down a few feet away from her, hitched his shoulders to straighten out the silver jacket, and lit a cigarette. "A little while after Bad News Quillan turned up just now," he went on, "a few things occurred to me. One of them was that a couple of years ago you and he were operating around Beldon at about the same time. I thought, well, maybe you knew each other; maybe not. And then —"

"Duke," Reetal said uncertainly, "just what are you talking about? I don't know —"

"Shut up." He reached over, tapped her knee lightly with his fingertips. "Of course, if you want to get slapped around, all right. Otherwise, don't interrupt again. Like I said, you're in luck; I don't have much time to spend here. You're getting off very easy. Now just listen.

"Bad News knew a lot about our operation and had a

story to explain that. If the story was straight, we couldn't touch him. But I was wondering about the two of you happening to be here on the Star again at the same time. A team maybe, eh? But he didn't mention you as being in on the deal. So what was the idea?

"And then, sweetheart, I remembered something else — and that tied it in. Know that little jolt people sometimes get when they're dropping off to sleep? Of course. Know another time they sometimes get it? When they're snapping back out of a Moment of Truth, eh? I remembered suddenly I'd felt a little jump like that while we were talking today. Might have been a reflex of some kind. Of course, it didn't occur to me at the time you could be pulling a lousy stunt like that on old Duke. Why take a chance on getting your neck broken?

"But, sweetheart, that's the tie-in! Quillan hasn't told it straight. He's got no backing. He's on his own. There's no gang outside somewhere that knows all about our little deal. He got his information right here, from you. And you got it from dumb old Duke, eh?"

"Duke," Reetal said quite calmly. "can I ask just one question?"

He stared bleakly at her a moment, then grinned. "It's my night to be big-hearted, I guess. Go ahead."

"I'm not trying to argue. But it simply doesn't make sense. If I learned about this operation you're speaking of from you, what reason could I have to feed you Truth in the first place? There'd be almost a fifty-fifty chance that you'd spot it immediately. Why should I take such a risk? Don't you see?"

Fluel shrugged, dropped his cigarette and ground it carefully into the carpet with the tip of his shoe.

"You'll start answering those questions yourself almost

immediately, sweetheart! Let's not worry about that now. Let me finish. Something happened to Movaine couple of hours ago. Nobody's fault. And something else happened to Marras Cooms just now. That puts me in charge of the operation here. Nice! isn't it? When we found Cooms lying in the hall with a hole through his stupid head, I told Baldy Perk it looked like Bad News had thrown in with the Star boys and done it. Know Baldy? He's Cooms' personal gun. Not what you'd call bright, and he's mighty hot now about Cooms. I left him in charge on our level, with orders to get Quillan the next time he shows up there. Well and good. The boys know Bad News' rep too well to try asking him questions. They won't take chances with him. They'll just gun him down together the instant they see him."

He paused to scuff his shoe over the mark the cigarette had left on the carpet, went on, "But there's Nome Lancion now. He kind of liked Cooms, and he might get suspicious. When there's a sudden vacancy in the organization like that, Nome takes a good look first at the man next in line. He likes to be sure the facts are as stated.

"So now you know the kind of answers from you I want to hear go down on the recorder, sweetheart. And be sure they sound right. I don't want to waste time on replays. You and Quillan were here on the Star. You got some idea of what was happening, realized you were due to be vaporized along with the rest of them after we left. There was no way out of the jam for you unless you could keep the operation from being carried out. You don't, by the way, mention getting any of that information from me. I don't want Lancion to think I'm beginning to get dopey. You and Quillan just cooked up this story, and he managed to get into the Executive Block. The idea being to knock off as many of the leaders as he could, and mess things up."

*   *   *

Fluel picked up the recorder, stood up, and placed it on the chair. "That's all you have to remember. You're a smart girl; you can fill in the detail any way you like. Now let's get started —"

She stared at him silently for instant, a muscle beginning to twitch in her cheek. "If I do that," she said, "if I give you a story Nome will like, what happens next?"

Fluel shrugged. "Just what you're thinking happens next. You're a dead little girl right now, Reetal. Might as well get used to the idea. You'd be dead anyhow four, five hours from now, so that shouldn't make too much difference. What makes a lot of difference is just how unpleasant the thing can get."

She drew a long breath. "Duke, I —"

"You're stalling, sweetheart."

"Duke, give me a break. I really didn't know a thing about this. I —"

He looked down at her for a moment. "I gave you a break," he said. "You've wasted it. Now we'll try it the other way. If we work a few squeals into the recording, that'll make it more convincing to Lancion. He'll figure little Reetal's the type who wouldn't spill a thing like that without a little pressure." He checked himself, grinned. "And that reminds me. When you're talking for the record, use your own voice."

"My own voice?" she half whispered.

"Nome will remember what you sound like — and I've heard that voice imitations are part of your stock in trade. You might think it was cute if Nome got to wondering after you were dead whether that really had been you talking. Don't try it, sweetheart."

He brought a glove out of his jacket pocket, slipped it over his left hand, flexing his fingers to work it into position. Reetal's eyes fastened on the rounded metal tips capping thumb, forefinger and middle finger of the glove. Her face went gray.

"Duke," she said. "No —"

"Shut up." He brought out a strip of transparent plastic, moved over to her. The gloved hand went into her hair, gripped it, turned her face up. He laid the plastic gag lengthwise over her mouth, pressed it down and released it. Reetal closed her eyes.

"That'll keep it shut," he said. "Now — " His right hand clamped about the back of her neck, forcing her head down and forward almost to her knees. The gloved left hand brushed her hair forwards, then its middle finger touched the skin at a point just above her shoulder blades.

"Right there," Fluel said. The finger stiffened, drove down.

Reetal jerked violently, twisted, squirmed sideways, wrists straining against the grip of the armrests. Her breath burst out of her nostrils, followed by squeezed, whining noises. The metal-capped finger continued to grind savagely against the nerve center it had found.

"Thirty," Fluel said finally. He drew his hand back, pulled her upright again, peeled the gag away from her lips. "Only thirty seconds, sweetheart. Think you'd sooner play along now?"

Reetal's head nodded.

"Fine. Give you a minute to steady up. This doesn't really waste much time, you see — " He took up the recorder, sat down on the chair again, watching her. She was breathing raggedly and shallowly, eyes wide and incredulous. She didn't look at him.

The Duke lit another cigarette.

"Incidentally," he observed, "if you were stalling because you hoped old Bad News might show up, forget it. If the boys haven't gunned him down by now, he's tied up on a job the commodore gave him to do. He'll be busy another hour or two on that. He —"

He checked himself. A central section of the wall paneling across the room from him had just dilated open. Old Bad News stood in the concealed suite portal, Rest Warden Kinmarten slung across his shoulder.

Both men moved instantly. Fluel's long legs bounced him sideways out of the chair, right hand darting under his coat, coming out with a gun. Quillan turned to the left to get Kinmarten out of the way. The big Miam Devil seemed to jump into his hand. Both guns spoke together.

Fluel's gun thudded to the carpet. The Duke said, "Ah-aa-ah!" in a surprised voice, rolled up his eyes, and followed the gun down.

Quillan said, stunned, "He was fast! I felt that one parting my hair."

He became very solicitous then — after first ascertaining that Fluel had left the Executive Block unaccompanied, on personal business. He located a pain killer spray in Reetal's bedroom and applied it to the bruised point below the back of her neck. She was just beginning to relax gratefully, as the warm glow of the spray washed out the pain and the feeling of paralysis, when Kinmarten, lying on the carpet nearby, began to stir and mutter.

Quillan hastily put down the spray.

"Watch him!" he cautioned. "I'll be right back. If he sits up, yell. He's a bit wild at the moment. If he wakes up and sees the Duke lying there, he'll start climbing the walls."

"What — " Reetal began. But he was gone down the hall.

He returned immediately with a glass of water, went down on one knee beside Kinmarten, slid an arm under the rest warden's shoulder, and lifted him to a sitting position.

"Wake up, old pal!" he said loudly. "Come on, wake up! Got something good for you here —"

"What are you giving him?" Reetal asked, cautiously massaging the back of her neck.

"Knockout drops. I already had to lay him out once. We want to lock him up with his wife now, and if he comes to and tells her what's happened, they'll both be out of their minds by the time we come to let them out —"

He interrupted himself. Kinmarten's eyelids were fluttering. Quillan raised the glass to his lips. "Here you are, pal," he said in a deep, soothing voice. "Drink it! It'll make you feel a lot better."

Kinmarten swallowed obediently, swallowed again. His eyelids stopped fluttering. Quillan lowered him back to the floor.

"That ought to do it," he said.

"What," Reetal asked, "did happen? The Duke —"

"Tell you as much as I can after we get Kinmarten out of the way. I have to get back to the Executive Block. Things are sort of teetering on the edge there." He jerked his head at Fluel's body. "I want to know about him, too, of course. Think you can walk now?"

Reetal groaned. "I can try," she said.

They found Solvey Kinmarten dissolved in tears once more. She flung herself on her husband's body when Quillan placed him on the bed. "What have those *beasts* done to Brock?" she demanded fiercely.

"Nothing very bad," Quillan said soothingly. "He's, um,

under sedation at the moment, that's all. We've got him away from them now, and he's safe . . . look at it that way. You stay here and take care of him. We'll have the whole deal cleared up before morning, doll. Then you can both come out of hiding again." He gave her an encouraging wink.

"I'm so very grateful to both of you —"

"No trouble, really. But we'd better get back to work on the thing."

"Heck," Quillan said a few seconds later, as he and Reetal came out on the other side of the portal, "I feel like hell about those two. Nice little characters! Well, if the works blow up, they'll never know it."

"*We'll* know it," Reetal said meaningly. "Start talking."

He rattled through a brief account of events in the Executive Block, listened to her report on the Duke's visit, scratched his jaw reflectively.

"That might help!" he observed. "They're about ready to jump down each other's throats over there right now. A couple more pushes — " He stood staring down at the Duke's body for a moment. Blood soiled the back of the silver jacket, seeping out from a tear above the heart area. Quillan bent down, got his hands under Fluel's armpits, hauled the body upright.

Reetal asked, startled, "What are you going to do with it?"

"Something useful, I think. And wouldn't that shock the Duke . . . the first time he's been of any use to anybody. Zip through the Star's ComWeb directory, doll, and get me the call symbol for Level Four of the Executive Block!"

*　　　*　　　*

Solvey Kinmarten dimmed the lights a trifle in the bedroom, went back to Brock, rearranged the pillows under his head, and bent down to place her lips tenderly to the large bruises on his forehead and the side of his jaw. Then she brought a chair up beside the bed, and sat down to watch him.

Perhaps a minute later, there was a slight noise behind her. Startled, she glanced around, saw something huge, black and shapeless moving swiftly across the carpet of the room toward her.

Solvey quietly fainted.

"Sure you know what to say?" Quillan asked.

Reetal moistened her lips. "Just let me go over it in my mind once more." She was sitting on the floor, on the right side of the ComWeb stand, her face pale and intent. "You know," she said, "this makes me feel a little queasy somehow, Quillan! And suppose they don't fall for it?"

"They'll fall for it!" Quillan was on his knees in front of the stand, supporting Fluel's body, which was sprawled half across it, directly before the lit vision screen. An outflung arm hid the Duke's face from the screen. "You almost had *me* thinking I was listening to Fluel when you did the takeoff on him this evening. A dying man can be expected to sound a little odd, anyway." He smiled at her encouragingly. "Ready now?"

Reetal nodded nervously, cleared her throat.

Quillan reached across Fluel, tapped out Level Four's call symbol on the instrument, ducked back down below the stand. After a moment, there was a click.

Reetal produced a quavering, agonized groan. Somebody else gasped.

"*Duke!*" Baldy Perkshouted. "What's happened?"

"Baldy Perk!" Quillan whispered quickly.

Reetal stammered hoarsely, "The c-c-commodore, Baldy! Shot me . . . shot Marras! They're after . . . Quillan . . . now!"

"I thought Bad News . . ." Baldy sounded stunned.

"Was w-wrong, Baldy," Reetal croaked. "Bad News . . . with us! Bad News . . . pal! The c-c-comm —"

Beneath the ComWeb stand the palm of Quillan's right hand thrust sharply up and forward. The stand tilted, went crashing back to the floor. Fluel's body lurched over with it. The vision screen shattered. Baldy's roaring question was cut off abruptly.

"Great stuff, doll!" Quillan beamed, helping Reetal to her feet. "You sent shudders down my back!"

"Down mine, too!"

"I'll get him out of here now. Ditch him in one of the shut-off sections. Then I'll get back to the Executive Block. If Ryter's thought to look into Kinmarten's room, they'll really be raving on both sides there now!"

"Is that necessary?" Reetal asked. "For you to go back, I mean. Somebody besides Fluel might have become suspicious of you by now."

"Ryter might," Quillan agreed "He's looked like the sharpest of the lot right from the start. But we'll have to risk that. We've got all the makings of a shooting war there now but we've got to make sure it gets set off before somebody thinks of comparing notes. If I'm around, I'll keep jolting at their nerves."

"I suppose you're right. Now, our group —"

Quillan nodded. "No need to hold off on that any longer, the way things are moving. Get on another ComWeb and start putting out those Mayday messages right now! As soon as you've rounded the boys up —"

"That might," Reetal said, "take a little less than an hour."

"Fine. Then move them right into the Executive Block. With just a bit of luck, one hour from now should land them in the final stages of a beautiful battle on the upper levels. Give them my description and Ryter's, so we don't have accidents."

"Why Ryter's?"

"Found out he was the boy who took care of the bomb-planting detail. We want him alive. The others mightn't know where it's been tucked away. Heraga says the clerical staff and technicians in there are all wearing the white Star uniforms. Anyone else who isn't in one of those uniforms is fair game — " He paused. "Oh, and tip them off about the Hlat. God only knows what that thing will be doing when the ruckus starts."

"What about sending a few men in through the fifth level portal, the one you've unplugged?"

Quillan considered, shook his head "No. Down on the ground level is where we want them. They'd have to portal there again from the fifth, and a portal is too easy to seal off and defend. Now let's get a blanket or something to tuck Fluel into. I don't want to feel conspicuous if I run into somebody on the way."

5

Quillan emerged cautiously from the fifth portal in the Executive Block a short while later, came to a sudden stop just outside it. In the big room beyond the entry hall, the door of the baited cubicle was closed and the life-indicator on the door showed a bright steady green glow.

Quillan stared at it a moment, looking somewhat surprised, then went quietly into the room and bent to study the cubicle's instruments. A grin spread slowly over his face. The trap had been sprung. He glanced at the deep-rest setting and turned it several notches farther down.

"Happy dreams, Lady Pendrake!" he murmured. "That takes care of you. What an appetite! And now —"

As the Level Four portal dilated open before him, a gun blazed from across the hall. Quillan flung himself out and down, rolled to the side, briefly aware of a litter of bodies and tumbled furniture farther up the hall. Then he was flat on the carpet, gun out before him, pointing back at the overturned, ripped couch against the far wall from which the fire had come.

A hoarse voice bawled, "Bad News — hold it!"

Quillan hesitated, darting a glance right and left. Men lying about everywhere, the furnishings a shambles. "That you, Baldy?" he asked.

"Yeah," Baldy Perk half sobbed. "I'm hurt —"

"What happened?"

"*Star* gang jumped us. Portaled in here — spitballs and riot guns! Bad News, we're clean wiped out! Everyone that was on this level —"

Quillan stood up, holstering the gun, went over to the couch and moved it carefully away from the wall. Baldy was crouched behind it, kneeling on the blood-soaked carpet, gun in his right hand. He lifted a white face, staring eyes, to Quillan.

"Waitin' for 'em to come back," he muttered. "Man, I'm not for long! Got hit twice. Near passed out a couple of times already."

"What about your boys on guard downstairs?"

"Same thing there, I guess . . . or they'd have showed up. They got Cooms and the Duke, too! Man, it all happened fast!"

"And the crew on the freighter?"

"Dunno about them."

"You know the freighter's call number?"

"Huh? Oh, yeah. Sure. Never thought of that," Baldy said wearily. He seemed dazed now.

"Let's see if you can stand."

Quillan helped the big man to his feet. Baldy hadn't bled too much outwardly, but he seemed to have estimated his own condition correctly. He wasn't for long. Quillan slid an arm under his shoulders.

"Where's a ComWeb?" he asked.

Baldy blinked about. "Passage there — " His voice was beginning to thicken.

The ComWeb was in the second room up the passage. Quillan eased Perk into the seat before it. Baldy's head lolled heavily forward, like a drunken man's "What's the number?" Quillan asked.

Baldy reflected a few seconds. blinking owlishly at the instrument, then told him. Quillan tapped out the number, flicked on the vision screen, then stood aside and back, beyond the screen's range.

"Yeah, Perk?" a voice said some seconds later. "Hey, *Perk* . . . Perk, what's with ya?"

Baldy spat blood, grinned. "Shot — " he said.

"*What?*"

"Yeah." Baldy scowled, blinking. "Now, lessee — Oh, yeah. Star gang's gonna jump ya! Watch it!"

"What?"

"Yeah, watch — " Baldy coughed, laid his big head

slowly down face forward on the ComWeb stand, and stopping moving.

"Perk! Man, wake up! Perk!"

Quillan quietly took out the gun, reached behind the stand and blew the ComWeb apart. He wasn't certain what the freighter's crew would make of the sudden break in the connection, but they could hardly regard it as reassuring. He made a brief prowl then through the main sections of the level. Evidence everywhere of a short and furious struggle, a struggle between men panicked and enraged almost beyond any regard for self-preservation. It must have been over in minutes. He found that the big hall portal to the ground level had been sealed, whether before or after the shooting he couldn't know. There would have been around twenty members of the Brotherhood on the level. None of them had lived as long as Baldy Park, but they seemed to have accounted for approximately an equal number of the Star's security force first.

F ive Star men came piling out of the fifth level portal behind him a minute or two later, Ryter in the lead. Orca behind Ryter. All five held leveled guns.

"You won't need the hardware," Quillan assured them. "It's harmless enough now. Come on in."

They followed him silently up to the cubicle, stared comprehendingly at dials and indicators. "The thing's back inside there, all right!" Ryter said. He looked at Quillan. "Is this where you've been all the time?"

"Sure. Where else?" The others were forming a half-circle about him, a few paces back.

"Taking quite a chance with that Hlat, weren't you?" Ryter remarked.

"Not too much. I thought of something." Quillan indicated the outportal in the hall. "I had my back against that. A portal's space-break, not solid matter. It couldn't come at me from behind. And if it attacked from any other angle" — he tapped the holstered Miam Devil lightly, and the gun in Orca's hand jerked upward a fraction of an inch — "There aren't many animals that can swallow more than a bolt or two from that baby and keep coming."

There was a moment's silence. Then Orca said thoughtfully, "That would work!"

"Did it see you?" Ryter asked.

"It couldn't have. First I saw of it, it was sailing out from that corner over there. It slammed in after that chunk of sea beef so fast, it shook the cubicle. And that was that." He grinned. "Well, most of our troubles should be over now!"

One of the men gave a brief, nervous laugh. Quillan looked at him curiously. "Something, chum?"

Ryter shook his head. "Something is right! Come on downstairs again, Bad News. This time we have news for you —"

The Brotherhood guards on the ground level had been taken by surprise and shot down almost without losses for the Star men. But the battle on the fourth level had cost more than the dead left up there. An additional number had returned with injuries that were serious enough to make them useless for further work.

"It's been expensive," Ryter admitted. "But one more attack by the Hlat would have left me with a panicked mob on my hands. If we'd realized it was going to trap itself —"

"I wasn't so sure that would work either," Quillan said. "Did you get Kinmarten back?"

"Not yet. The chances are he's locked up somewhere on the fourth level. Now the Hlat's out of the way, some of the men have gone back up there to look for him. If Cooms thought he was important enough to start a fight over, I want him back."

"How about the crew on the Beldon ship?" Quillan asked. "Have they been cleaned up?"

"No," Ryter said. "We'll have to do that now, of course."

"How many of them?"

"Supposedly twelve. And that's probably what it is."

"If they know or suspect what's happened," Quillan said, "twelve men can give a boarding party in a lock a remarkable amount of trouble."

Ryter shrugged irritably. "I know, but there isn't much choice. Lancion's bringing in the other group on the *Camelot*. We don't want to have to handle both of them at the same time."

"How are you planning to take the freighter?"

"When the search party comes back down, we'll put every man we can spare from guard duty here on the job. They'll be instructed to be careful about it . . . if they can wind up the matter within the next several hours, that will be early enough. We can't afford too many additional losses now. But we should come out with enough men to take care of Lancion and handle the shipment of Hlats. And that's what counts."

"Like me to take charge of the boarding party?" Quillan inquired. "That sort of thing's been a kind of specialty of mine."

Ryter looked at him without much expression on his face. "I understand that," he said. "But perhaps it would be better if you stayed up here with us."

*   *   *

The search party came back down ten minutes later. They'd looked through every corner of the fourth level. Kinmarten wasn't there, either dead or alive. But one observant member of the group had discovered, first, that the Duke of Fluel was also not among those present, and, next, that one of the four outportals on the level had been unsealed. The exit on which the portal was found to be set was in a currently unused hall in the General Offices building on the other side of the Star. From that hall, almost every other section of the Star was within convenient portal range.

None of the forty-odd people working in the main control office on the ground level had actually witnessed any shooting; but it was apparent that a number of them were uncomfortably aware that something quite extraordinary must be going on. They were a well-disciplined group, however. An occasional uneasy glance toward one of the armed men lounging along the walls, some anxious faces, were the only noticeable indications of tension. Now and then, there was a brief, low-pitched conversation at one of the desks.

Quillan stood near the center of the office, Ryter and Orca a dozen feet from him on either side. Four Star guards were stationed along the walls. From the office one could see through a large doorspace cut through both sides of a hall directly into the adjoining transmitter room. Four more guards were in there. Aside from the men in the entrance hall and at the subspace portal, what was available at the moment of Ryter's security force was concentrated at this point.

The arrangement made considerable sense; and Quillan gave no sign of being aware that the eyes of the guards shifted to him a little more frequently than to any other point in the office, or that none of them had moved his hand very far away from his gun since they had come in here. But that also made sense. In the general tension area of the Executive Block's ground level, a specific point of tension — highly charged though undetected by the noninvolved personnel — was the one provided by the presence of Bad News Quillan here. Ryter was more than suspicious by now; the opened portal on the fourth level, the disappearance of Kinmarten and the Duke, left room for a wide variety of speculations. Few of those speculations could be very favorable to Bad News. Ryter obviously preferred to let things stand as they were until the Beldon freighter was taken and the major part of his group had returned from the subspace sections of the Star. At that time, Bad News could expect to come in for some very direct questioning by the security chief.

The minutes dragged on. Under the circumstances, a glance at his watch could be enough to bring Ryter's uncertainties up to the explosion point, and Quillan also preferred to let things stand as they were for the moment. But he felt reasonably certain that over an hour had passed since he'd left Reetal; and so far there had been no hint of anything unusual occurring in the front part of the building. The murmur of voices in the main control office continued to eddy about him. There were indications that in the transmitter room across the hall messages had begun to be exchanged between the Star and the approaching liner.

A man sitting at a desk near Quillan stood up presently, went out into the hall and disappeared. A short while later, the white-suited figure returned and picked up the interrupted work. Quillan's glance went over the clerk, shifted on. He felt something tighten up swiftly inside him. There was a considerable overall resemblance, but *that* wasn't the man who had left the office.

Another minute or two went by. Then two other uniformed figures appeared at the opening to the hall, a sparse elderly man, a blond girl. They stood there talking earnestly together for some seconds, then came slowly down the aisle toward Quillan. It appeared to be an argument about some detail of her work. The girl frowned, stubbornly shaking her head. Near Quillan they separated, started off into different sections of the office. The girl, glancing back, still frowning, brushed against Ryter. She looked up at him. startled.

"I'm sorry," she said.

Ryter scowled irritably, started to say something, suddenly appeared surprised. Then his eyes went blank and his knees buckled under him.

The clerk sitting at the nearby desk whistled shrilly.

Quillan wheeled, gun out and up, toward the wall behind him. The two guards there were still lifting their guns. The Miam Devil grunted disapprovingly twice, and the guards went down. Noise crashed from the hall . . . heavy sporting rifles. He turned again, saw the two other guards stumbling backward along the far wall. Feminine screaming erupted around the office as the staff dove out of sight behind desks, instrument stands and filing cabinets. The elderly man stood above Orca, a sap in his hand and a pleased smile on his face.

In the hallway, four white-uniformed men had swung about and were pointing blazing rifles into the transmitter room. The racketing of the gunfire ended abruptly and the rifles were lowered again. The human din in the office began to diminish, turned suddenly into a shocked, strained silence. Quillan realized the blond girl was standing at his elbow.

"Did you get the rest of them?" he asked quickly, in a low voice.

"Everyone who was on this level," Reetal told him. "There weren't many of them."

"I know. But there's a sizable batch still in the subspace section. If we can get the bomb disarmed, we'll just leave them sealed up there. How long before you can bring Ryter around?"

"He'll be able to talk in five minutes."

6

Quillan had been sitting for some little while in a very comfortable chair in what had been the commodore's personal suite on the Seventh Star, broodingly regarding the image of the *Camelot* in a huge wall screen. The liner was still over two hours' flight away but would arrive on schedule. On the Star, at least in the normspace section, everything was quiet; and in the main control offices and in the transmitter room normal working conditions had been restored.

A room portal twenty feet away opened suddenly, and Reetal Destone stepped out.

"So there you are!" she observed.

Quillan looked mildly surprised then grinned. "I'd hate to have to try to hide from you!" he said.

"Hm-m-m!" said Reetal. She smiled. "What are you drinking?"

He nodded at an open liquor cabinet near the screen. "Velladon was leaving some excellent stuff behind. Join me?"

"Hm-m-m." She went to the cabinet, looked over the bottles, made her selection and filled a glass. "One has the impression," she remarked, "that you *were* hiding from me."

"One does? I'd have to be losing my cotton-picking mind —"

"Not necessarily." Reetal brought the drink over to his chair, sat down on the armrest with it. "You might just have a rather embarrassing problem to get worked out before you give little Reetal a chance to start asking questions about it."

Quillan looked surprised. "What gave you that notion?"

"Oh," Reetal said, "adding things up gave me that motion . . . Care to hear what the things were?"

"Go ahead, doll."

"First," said Reetal, "I understand that a while ago, after you'd first sent me off to do some little job for you, you were in the transmitter room having a highly private — shielded and scrambled — conversation with somebody on board the *Camelot*."

"Why, yes," Quillan said. "I was talking to the ship's security office. They're arranging to have a Federation police boat pick up what's left of the commodore's boys and the Brotherhood in the subspace section."

"And that," said Reetal, "is where that embarrassing little problem begins. Next, I noticed, as I say, that you were showing this tendency to avoid a chance for a private talk between us. And after thinking about that for a little, and also about a few other things which came to mind at around that time, I went to see Ryter."

"Now why — ?"

Reetal ran her fingers soothingly through his hair. "Let me finish, big boy. I found Ryter and Orca in a highly nervous condition. And do you know why they're nervous? They're convinced that some time before the *Camelot* gets here, you're going to do them both in."

"Hm-m-m," said Quillan.

"Ryter," she went on, "besides being nervous, is also very bitter. In retrospect, he says, it's all very plain what you've done here. You and your associates — a couple of tough boys named Hagready and Boltan, and others not identified — are also after these Hlats. The Duke made some mention of that, too, you remember. The commodore and Ryter bought the story you told them because a transmitter check produced the information that Hagready and Boltan had, in fact, left their usual work areas and gone off on some highly secret business about a month ago.

"Ryter feels that your proposition — to let your gang in on the deal for twenty per cent, or else — was made in something less than good faith. He's concluded that when you learned of the operation being planned by Velladon and the Brotherhood, you and your pals decided to obstruct them and take the Hlats for delivery to Yaco yourselves, without cutting anybody in. He figures that someone like Hagready or Boltan is coming in on the *Camelot* with a flock of sturdy henchmen to do just that. You, personally, rushed to the Seventh Star to interfere as much as you could here. Ryter admits reluctantly that you did an extremely good job of interfering. He says it's now obvious that every move you made since you showed up had the one purpose of setting the Star group and the Brotherhood at each other's throats. And now that they've practically wiped each other out, you and your associates can go on happily with your original plans.

"But, of course, you can't do that if Ryter and Orca are picked up alive by the Federation cops. The boys down in the subspace section don't matter; they're ordinary gunhands and all they know is that you were somebody who showed up on the scene. But Ryter could, and certainly would, talk —"

"Ah, he's too imaginative," Quillan said, taking a swallow of his drink. "I never heard of the Hlats before I got here. As I told you, I'm on an entirely different kind of job at the moment. I had to make up some kind of story to get an in with the boys, that's all."

"So you're not going to knock those two weasels off?"

"No such intentions. I don't mind them sweating about it till the Feds arrive, but that's it."

"What about Boltan and Hagready?"

"What about them? I did happen to know that if anyone started asking questions about those two, he'd learn that neither had been near his regular beat for close to a month."

"I'll bet!" Reetal said cryptically.

"What do you mean by that?"

"Hm-m-m," she said. "Bad News Quillan! A really tough boy, for sure. You know, I didn't believe for an instant that you were after the Hlats —"

"Why not?"

Reetal said, "I've been on a couple of operations with you, and you'd be surprised how much I've picked up about you from time to time on the side. Swiping a shipment of odd animals and selling them to Yaco, that could be Bad News, in character. Selling a couple of hundred human beings — like Brock and Solvey Kinmarten — to go along with the animals to an outfit like Yaco would not be in character."

"So I have a heart of gold," Quillan said.

"So you fell all over your own big feet about half a minute ago!" Reetal told him. "Bad News Quillan — with no interest whatsoever in the Hlats — still couldn't afford to let Ryter live to talk about him to the Feds, big boy!"

Quillan looked reflective for a moment. "Dirty trick!" he observed. "For that, you might freshen up my glass."

Reetal took both glasses over to the liquor cabinet, freshened them up, and settled down on the armrest of the chair again. "So there we're back to the embarrassing little problem," she said.

"Ryter?"

"No, idiot. We both know that Ryter is headed for Rehabilitation. Fifteen years or so of it, at a guess. The problem is little Reetal who has now learned a good deal more than she was ever intended to learn. Does she head for Rehabilitation, too?"

Quillan took a swallow of his drink and set the glass down again. "Are you suggesting," he inquired, "that I might be, excuse the expression, a cop?"

Reetal patted his head. "Bad News Quillan! Let's look back at his record. What do we find? A shambles, mainly. Smashed-up organizations, outfits, gangs. Top-level crooks with suddenly vacant expressions and unexplained holes in their heads. Why go on? The name is awfully well earned! And nobody realizing anything because the ones who do realize it suddenly . . . well, where *are* Boltan and Hagready at the moment?"

Quillan sighed. "Since you keep bringing it up — Hagready played it smart, so he's in Rehabilitation. Be cute if Ryter ran into him there some day. Pappy Boltan didn't want to play it smart. I'm not enough of a philosopher to make a guess at where he might be at present. But I knew he wouldn't be talking."

"All right," Reetal said, "we've got that straight. Bad News is Intelligence of some kind. Federation maybe, or maybe one of the services. It doesn't matter, really, I suppose. Now, what about me?"

He reached out and tapped his glass with a fingertip. "That about you, doll. You filled it. I'm drinking it. I may not think quite as fast as you do, but I still think. Would I take a drink from a somewhat lawless and very clever lady who really believed I had her lined up for Rehabilitation? Or who'd be at all likely to blab out something that would ruin an old pal's reputation?"

Reetal ran her fingers through his hair again. "I noticed the deal with the drink," she said. "I guess I just wanted to hear you say it. You don't tell on me, I don't tell on you. Is that it?"

"That's it," Quillan said. "What Ryter and Orca want to tell the Feds doesn't matter. It stops there; the Feds will have the word on me before they arrive. By the way, did you go wake up the Kinmartens yet?"

"Not yet," Reetal said. "Too busy getting the office help soothed down and back to work."

"Well, let's finish these drinks and go do that, then. The little doll's almost bound to be asleep by now, but she might still be sitting there biting nervously at her pretty knuckles."

Major Heslet Quillan, of Space Scout Intelligence, was looking unhappy. "We're still searching for them everywhere," he explained to Klayung, "but it's a virtual certainty that the Hlat got them shortly before it was trapped."

Klayung, a stringy, white-haired old gentleman, was an operator of the Psychology Service, in charge of the shipment of Hlats the *Camelot* had brought in. He and Quillan were waiting in the vestibule of the Seventh Star's rest cubicle vaults for Lady Pendrake's cubicle to be brought over from the Executive Block.

Klayung said reflectively, "Couldn't the criminals with

whom you were dealing here have hidden the couple away somewhere?"

Quillan shook his head. "There's no way they could have located them so quickly. I made half a dozen portal switches when I was taking Kinmarten to the suite. It would take something with a Hlat's abilities to follow me over that route and stay undetected. And it must be an unusually cunning animal to decide to stay out of sight until I'd led it where it wanted to go."

"Oh, they're intelligent enough," Klayung agreed absently. "Their average basic I.Q. is probably higher than that of human beings. A somewhat different type of mentality, of course. Well, when the cubicle arrives, I'll question the Hlat and we'll find out."

Quillan looked at him. "Those control devices make it possible to hold two-way conversations with the things?"

"Not exactly," Klayung said. "You see, major, the government authorities who were concerned with the discovery of the Hlats realized it would be almost impossible to keep some information about them from getting out. The specimen which was here on the Star has been stationed at various scientific institutions for the past year; a rather large number of people were involved in investigating it and experimenting with it. In consequence, several little legends about them have been deliberately built up. The legends aren't entirely truthful, so they help to keep the actual facts about the Hlats satisfactorily vague."

"The Hlat-talker is such a legend. Actually, the device does nothing. The Hlats respond to telepathic stimuli, both among themselves and from other beings, eventually begin to correlate such stimuli with the meanings of human speech."

"Then you — " Quillan began.

"Yes. Eltak, their discoverer, was a fairly good natural telepath. If he hadn't been abysmally lazy, he might have been very good at it. I carry a variety of the Service's psionic knickknacks about with me, which gets me somewhat comparable results."

He broke off as the vestibule portal dilated widely. Lady Pendrake's cubicle floated. through, directed by two gravity crane operators behind it. Klayung stood up.

"Set it there for the present, please," he directed the operators. "We may call for you later if it needs to be moved again."

He waited until the portal had closed behind the men before walking over to the cubicle. He examined the settings and readings at some length.

"Hm-m-m, yes," he said, straightening finally. His expression became absent for a few seconds; then he went on. "I'm beginning to grasp the situation, I believe. Let me tell you a few things about the Hlats, major. For one, they form quite pronounced likes and dislikes. Eltak, for example, would have been described by most of his fellow men as a rather offensive person. But the Hlats actually became rather fond of him during the fifteen or so years he lived on their island.

"That's one point. The other has to do with their level of intelligence. We discovered on the way out here that our charges had gained quite as comprehensive an understanding of the functioning of the cubicles that had been constructed for them as any human who was not a technical specialist might do. And —"

He interrupted himself, stood rubbing his chin for a moment.

"Well, actually," he said, "that should be enough to prepare you for a look inside the Hlat's cubicle."

Quillan gave him a somewhat surprised glance. "I've been told it's ugly as sin," he remarked. "But I've seen some fairly revolting looking monsters before this."

Klayung coughed. "That's not exactly what I meant," he said. "I . . . well, let's just open the thing up. Would you mind, major?"

"Not at all." Quillan stepped over to the side of the cubicle, unlocked the door switch and pulled it over. They both moved back a few feet before the front of the cubicle. A soft humming came for some seconds from the door's mechanisms; then it suddenly swung open. Quillan stooped to glance inside, straightened instantly again, hair bristling.

"*Where is it?*" he demanded, the Miam Devil out in his hand.

Klayung looked at him thoughtfully. "Not very far away, I believe. But I can assure you, major, that it hasn't the slightest intention of attacking us — or anybody else — at present."

Quillan grunted, looked back into the cubicle. At the far end, the Kinmartens lay side by side, their faces composed. They appeared to be breathing regularly.

"Yes," Klayung said, "they're alive and unharmed." He rubbed his chin again. "And I think it would be best if we simply closed the cubicle now. Later we can call a doctor over from the hospital to put them under sedation before they're taken out. They've both had thoroughly unnerving experiences, and it would be advisable to awaken them gradually to avoid emotional shock."

He moved over to the side of the cubicle, turned the door switch back again. "And now for the rest of it," he said. "We may as well sit down again, major. This may take a little time."

*　　　*　　　*

"Let's look at the thing for a moment from the viewpoint of the Hlat," he resumed when he was once more comfortably seated. "Eltak's death took it by surprise. It hadn't at that point grasped what the situation in the Executive Block was like. It took itself out of sight for the moment, killing one of the gang leaders in the process, then began prowling about the various levels of the building, picking up information from the minds and conversation of the men it encountered. In a fairly short time, it learned enough to understand what was planned by the criminals; and it arrived at precisely your own conclusion . . . that it might be possible to reduce and demoralize the gangs to the extent that they would no longer be able to carry out their plan. It began a systematic series of attacks on them with that end in mind.

"But meanwhile you had come into the picture. The Hlat was rather puzzled by your motive at first because there appeared to be an extraordinary degree of discrepancy between what you were saying and what you were thinking. But after observing your activities for a while, it began to comprehend what you were trying to do. It realized that your approach was more likely to succeed than its own, and that further action on its side might interfere with your plans. But there remained one thing for it to do.

"I may tell you in confidence, major, that another legend which has been spread about these Hlats is their supposed inability to escape from the cubicles. Even their attendants are supplied with this particular bit of misinformation. Actually, the various force fields in the cubicles don't hamper them in the least. The cubicles are designed simply to protect the Hlats and keep them from being seen; and rest cubicles, of course, can be taken anywhere without arousing undue curiosity."

"You mentioned that the Kinmartens are very likable young people. The Hlat had the same feeling about them; they were the only human beings aside from Eltak with whose minds it had become quite familiar. There was no assurance at this point that the plans to prevent a bomb from being exploded in the Star would be successful, and the one place where human beings could hope to survive such an explosion was precisely the interior of the Hlat's cubicle, which had been constructed to safeguard its occupant against any kind of foreseeable accident.

"So the Hlat sprang your cubicle trap, removed the bait, carried the Kinmartens inside, and whipped out of the cubicle again before the rest current could take effect on it. It concluded correctly that everyone would decide it had been recaptured. After that, it moved about the Executive Block, observing events there and prepared to take action again if that appeared to be advisable. When you had concluded your operation successfully, it remained near the cubicle, waiting for me to arrive."

Quillan shook his head. "That's quite an animal!" he observed after some seconds. "You say it's in our general vicinity now?"

"Yes," Klayung said. "It followed the cubicle down here, and has been drifting about the walls of the vestibule while we . . . well, while I talked."

"Why doesn't it show itself?"

Klayung cleared his throat. "For two reasons," he said. "One is that rather large gun you're holding on your knees. It saw you use it several times, and after all the shooting in the Executive Block, you see —"

Quillan slid the Miam Devil into its holster. "Sorry," he said. "Force of habit, I guess. Actually, of course, I've understood for some minutes now that I wasn't . . . well, what's the other reason?"

"I'm afraid," Klayung said, "that you offended it with your remark about its appearance. Hlats may have their share of vanity. At any rate, it seems to be sulking."

"Oh," said Quillan. "Well, I'm sure," he went on rather loudly, "that it understands I received the description from a prejudiced source. I'm quite willing to believe it was highly inaccurate."

"Hm-m-m," said Klayung. "That seems to have done it, major. The wall directly across from us —"

Something like a ripple passed along the sidewall of the vestibule. Then the wall darkened suddenly, turned black. Quillan blinked, and the Hlat came into view. It hung, spread out like a spider, along half the length of the vestibule wall. Something like a huge, hairy amoeba in overall appearance, though the physical structures under the coarse, black pelt must be of very un-amoebalike complexity. No eyes were in sight, but Quillan had the impression of being regarded steadily. Here and there, along the edges and over the surface of the body, were a variety of flexible extensions.

Quillan stood up, hitched his gun belt into position, and started over toward the wall.

"Lady Pendrake," he said, "honored to meet you. Could we shake hands?"

www.ingramcontent.com/pod-product-compliance
Lightning Source LLC
Chambersburg PA
CBHW020646180626
46816CB00003B/1141